Dumb

Dumb

Skyy

www.urbanbooks.net

Urban Books, LLC
300 Farmingdale Road, NY-Route 109
Farmingdale, NY 11735

ISBN 13: 978-1-64556-614-4

First Mass Market Printing March 2024
First Trade Paperback Printing January 2023
Printed in the United States of America

10 9 8 7 6 5 4 3 2 1

Distributed by Kensington Publishing Corp.
Submit Orders to:
Customer Service
400 Hahn Road
Westminster, MD 21157-4627
Phone: 1-800-733-3000
Fax: 1-800-659-2436

Dedication

To the one who shan't be named:
You made me realize all the things I would never
want in a mate ever. Kick rocks.

&

For C. Brooks AKA For_Gotham,
The one who helped me realize what I truly want,
and desire in relationships. Because of you, I now
know what to require, and what I deserve. And if
what I want isn't reciprocated, it's not really for
me. I will always appreciate you for that.

This book is dedicated to all the people who were
dumb for someone at some time in their lives.
Here's to growth and realizing you deserve better.

Acknowledgments

Hey, folks:

Yeah, I know, it's been a long time. And yes, I know that this isn't the "Choices" book you guys want. To be honest, I didn't know if I would ever write another book, but I guess life had a different plan for me.

This book isn't my typical work. It's not about finding love or having great friendships. Honestly, this is a book about being very, VERY stupid for love. And yes, it's loosely based on something that happened to me. I can't believe I'm admitting this right now. However, a lot has been changed to protect the guilty. This was probably the lowest moment in my life. I look back now and say, "Seriously, Skyy, what the fuck were you thinking?" But writing truly can be one of the best forms of therapy.

When reading this book, there might be times you want to throw it across the room. You also might want to send me DMs to curse me out. It's okay. I'll accept that. What I truly hope is that someone will read this book, realize the situation they are currently in is way too familiar, and make changes to correct it. We all make mistakes when it comes to love, but correct the issues, heal from the pain, learn from the mistakes, and try to never repeat them again. That is a part I struggle with even to this day.

My sisters in thickness, Juanita Douglass, Tempress Wade, Jackie Mablin, JoAnn Townsend, and Shakira Luckett: I'm so happy to have met you and to have y'all in my life.

Now to the sappy stuff:

To My Super Fun Friends:

MeShanna Jones, Laterica Rose, LaMisha Merrett, Candace Kid, Deborah Hosier, Sadiece Holland, Quiana Dixon, Craig Brewer, Jill Robinson, Tamera Banks, Tiffany Graham, Rayne Dunbar, Shawn Lee, Jeffrey Farmer, Chereny Woodard, Kiona Luster, Catherine Evans, Shahidah Jones.

This book is truly dedicated to all of you. I know you guys love me unconditionally, but that love also can be infuriating, simply because I do not make good decisions when it comes to love. You guys support me even when you know I'm headed down a bad path, you try to help me make better decisions and alert me of the red flags I ignore or can't see. You are always there to pick me up when I eventually fall from the bad love decisions I've made. And you are also not afraid to dish me the tough love I desperately need at times. I apologize for the amount of times you've had to pick me up off the ground or had to catch me from jumping off the cliff for people who never deserved a piece of my time, energy, and definitely not my love. I am grateful that you all have stuck by me, and I promise to be a better me from here on out.

I always name a song that I listened to most while writing. For this book, it's "What's It Like" by Jagged Edge. I wanna be in love. It's my right to be. And one day, I will be with someone who loves me the way I truly deserve.

Welcome to a story about me being a dumb bitch. Enjoy!

Preface

LIT bookstore was buzzing. The small bookstore was one of the two surviving independent bookstores in Memphis, Tennessee. I loved it not only because it boasted the largest African American book selection in the city with a strong emphasis on urban literature, but it also had the best coffee and food. It even held a large comic and manga section which I particularly loved. It quickly became the hangout spot for artists and literary nerds. With their success, they opened "The Den," the open space in the back of the building with a small stage. It was used for everything from meetings to open mic nights. But today, it was used for the main reason they created it: for author book releases and signings.

I watched the crack in the door of the small holding area for guests as the place filled up quickly. Women of all shapes and sizes, primarily Black, filed in, clinging to their newly purchased novels. Book clubs adorned their special colors or matching T-shirts and claimed their own sections for their members, greeting them as they walked in. Some women chatted about the book, comparing their thoughts, while others buried their heads in their copies, waiting for the event to start.

"Hey, hey, ready to do this?" Kasim Future, the owner of the establishment, walked into my room. Kasim was the epitome of "Earthy Sexy." His locs were perfectly manicured and hung down almost to his butt. He always had them wrapped in something, today, settling for a white kente cloth print, thick headband. He always dressed in earth tones, distressed jeans or pants, and button-down shirts that seemed to cling just right to his slender frame. He handed me an insulated coffee cup. "Chai tea with lemon, just the way you like it." Kasim smiled.

I took the cup and quickly took a sip. "I swear, Kasim, I don't know what you add to this, but it's heaven on earth."

"Why, thank you. Starbucks ain't got shit on me." We both laughed. "All right, I'm going to introduce you before the crowd has my head."

"All right, let's do this."

Kasim greeted a few women in passing as he walked onto the stage. The women immediately stopped what they were doing to focus on him, some eyeing him from head to toe. He turned the microphone on and tapped it twice to ensure it was working.

"All right, look at all these beautiful Nubian queens in the building today. I need to have more book signings with Paige if this is what I will get in my store. You ladies look amazing." He let them swoon for a spell before finishing his introduction. "Well, we all know why you are here. But first, let me welcome you all to LIT. The cafe is open, the coffee is brewing, and I can tell you the cinnamon rolls will make you wanna slap someone."

The women laughed but really wanted him to get on with the introduction. Kasim could tell they didn't care about anything he had to say. They were ready for what they came for.

"I'm not going to take any more time plugging the establishment. Y'all know the deal, so let's get on to the main event. Ever since this book dropped, I haven't been able to keep them on the shelves. And it only makes me even prouder that this queen is a hometown girl right here from the 9.0.1." The crowd clapped. "So without any further ado, ladies, and you four gentlemen, let's give it up for Paige."

I took a deep breath and another sip of my drink, then walked out of the small greenroom. The crowd burst into applause. It was a bit overwhelming. Kasim hugged me and handed me the mic. Then I took a seat on the stool.

"Wow, thank you so much for the warm applause." My voice trembled. "No matter how many of these I do, it's always a bit scary for me, so please, bear with me."

The crowd gave their verbal assurance that everything would be all right and that I could take my time.

"I know some of you wanted to hear me read from the book, but I'd rather hear from you. So, any questions?"

I hated doing book readings. As a writer, I prefer to hide behind my computer screen in the comfort of my own home. But with the success of this new book, my publishers insisted on a twenty-city book tour starting in Memphis. The success felt bittersweet. My entire life, I wanted to achieve this level of success. I'd been on the Essence bestsellers list before, but I was never number one or even top ten. Now, I sit in the Top Twenty with the *New York Times*, based on a book I wrote about one of the worst moments in my life. I was happy people were finding solace in my pain but hated it happened.

Hands shot up in the air. I pointed at a young woman with long red and black ombre, knotless braids hanging almost to her butt. She stood up and pulled her shirt that said, "*Break up with him.*" I chuckled to myself. I knew the shirt was from the podcast "*The Read.*" I had the same shirt.

"Paige, this book. Oh my God, gurl, it's everything! I have to know, how did you come up with this idea?"

I took a deep breath. I knew it was the question I would be asked the most. I had gone over my politically correct answer a thousand times. Finally, I decided that I couldn't tell the actual truth. How would people look at me if they knew this wasn't all some lavish fantasy made up in my mind? But standing in front of the room full of women, all eyes focused directly on me, I knew how I needed to answer.

"Well . . ."

I swallowed hard.

"The truth is, this book was created because it was not too long ago I was a dumb bitch and decided to write about it."

Chapter 1

Lightning flashed across the sky, brightening my room out of its darkness for fleeting moments. It had been an unusually wet couple of weeks for Memphis. The bipolar weather gave us monsoon-like rains instead of snow or ice. The rain pounded, jolting the windows that thudded against each drop, creating an extra layer of ambiance to go with the smooth soul sex playlist echoing through my room.

"Damn, yo' pussy is so fucking good." Derrick raised his head to kiss me on my lips. "Fuck, how is your pussy always so tight? You 'bout to make me cum."

I let out a soft moan. The moment he lowered his head again, I felt my eyes roll. It was the same banter he always did. It was cute when we first started this sexual relationship, but how often did I need to hear my pussy was "tight"? I really wanted him to get over it already. Derrick's massive body was only matched by his big dick. Six foot three, dark and average looking, it had been four years of our random romps in the bed. The first time we fucked, it was the best sex I had ever had. Now, I just wanted it to end.

I regretted the decision to allow him to come over. I had been doing just fine with the array of sex toys I had purchased over the last year. Between my rose, silver bullets, and magic wand, I didn't think I needed a man anymore. I didn't know if it was the rain or just a simple bout of loneliness, but when Derrick texted me, I actually answered.

I needed this to end. I pushed Derrick over on his back and climbed on top. He grabbed my mounds of flesh. He was an avid lover of big girls, which was a total turn-on to me at the beginning of our situationship. But things had changed over the last few years. One thing was that Derrick had let himself go some. His love of beer and liquor had turned into a round beer belly that I definitely wasn't a fan of. I knew I was wrong to have an issue with another plus-size person. It was just slightly uncomfortable having sex with him at his larger size. Luckily, his massive penis and killer tongue typically did the trick anyway.

I put my hands on his chest, moving my hips in a circular motion. He massaged my flesh he had gripped between his two big hands. I could feel the hard spots from calluses resulting from his construction job. I had told him a million times to get a manicure, but his toxic masculinity wouldn't let him do things he deemed "girly."

I closed my eyes, throwing my head back as I gripped his dick with my strong eagle-Kegel skills. He let out a moan as his bottom lip fell open. Derrick closed his eyes and grabbed my sides tight as his body tensed up. I knew what was coming. I gripped and gyrated my hips until his moan turned into a deep, quivering roar.

"Ah, shit." Derrick picked me up with ease, placing me on the empty side of my king-sized bed. I sat there, basking in my triumph of making him orgasm. Then he sat on the side of the bed, struggling to catch his breath. He was struggling more than usual. It was a bit worrisome to me.

"Are you all right?" I put my hand on his back.

"Yeah, I'm good. You and your pussy trying to take me outta this junt." Finally, he stood up.

I laughed. "Naw, just proving a point. I think that's one point for Paige." I smiled. For years, his stamina was unmatched. I typically ended up tapping out. But these last few times, I was the one in control.

"All right," he said. I watched as he slowly moved around, picking up each piece of clothing. "I'll give you that. You fucked the shit out of me tonight. One point for Paige."

Derrick walked into my master bathroom and closed the door. I could hear the shower turn on. I frowned. I set out his usual facecloth and towel, the same as I did at my apartment. But for some reason, now at my new home, he wanted to take a real shower instead of his usual sink ho bath.

This was his first time in my new home. I was proud of my *Fortress of Solitude*, which I had recently purchased a few months earlier. I looked around my large bedroom. It was the bedroom of my dreams . . . large and spacious. My big king bed sat against the back middle wall as the statement piece I always dreamed it would be. I was so happy to be out of apartments. I loved everything about my house, especially my bedroom. It was the place I found the most solace after a long day.

The water turned off, bringing me back from my happy daydream. I quickly grabbed my oversized sleep shirt and threw it over my head. Derrick was the first man who made me feel completely comfortable in my skin as a big woman. He loved big women and was the first man to insist I be completely naked during sex, but I still wasn't overly comfortable being naked in front of him when we weren't between the sheets.

The door opened, and he walked out with my towel rubbing his dick. "Paige, that damn shower. Yeah, I need one of those." I knew exactly what he meant. Another favorite thing in my bedroom was my bathroom and shower, which were also very spacious. My walk-in shower boasted two showerheads, a handheld shower arm extension, and a large, square showerhead with multiple functions. I currently had it set on a monsoon feature, which provided a strong rainwater flow.

"You're welcome." I rolled my eyes. "You just decided to help yourself, I see."

Derrick paused. "Damn, I can't use your fancy shower?"

I nodded. "Of course, you can. You've just never done it before."

"Well," Derrick wiped the brow of his forehead with the towel. His naked body glistened from the dampness. "I saw that shower and just had to check it out. You really did the damn thing with this house." I had to agree with him on that.

This house was my gift to me after my last book hit the Essence bestsellers list. After three consecutive books making it to the Top Ten, I finally decided to take some of my hard-earned money and splurge on my dream home. Three bedrooms, an office, a living room, and my own little nerdy lair. I loved everything about my home.

"Well, I'm glad you enjoyed it," I said as I watched him dress.

"Yeah, I really did."

I continued to watch as he buckled his pants. Derrick waited 'til after he put on his shoes to put on his shirt. I never quite understood why he always did that. We had been doing our thing for so long that I couldn't help but notice his usual routines.

"Derrick, do you know we have been doing whatever this is for almost five years?"

He paused. "Damn, has it *really* been that long?"

I nodded. "I mean, should we go out and celebrate our fuck-aversary?" I smirked.

Derrick threw his shirt over his head. "I'll pass."

His response wasn't surprising, but for some reason, it bothered me. It dawned on me that we had never been out in public in five years. From the moment he fell into my DMs, it was his place or mine. Although sometimes, we would watch a little TV or play a video game before smashing, dinner and movies never were in the equation. I don't know why this was suddenly bothering me. I shook off the strange feelings. After all, I knew what this was. Derrick wasn't someone to date; he was just someone to fuck.

I pulled myself out of bed to walk him to the door. I suddenly felt this odd sense of regret. I just wanted him gone. Derrick went in for a hug. I gently patted him on the back, pulling away quickly. He looked at me. It was apparent he could feel the attitude, but he didn't question it at all.

"See ya later, Paige." He opened the door. "Hit me when you want another session."

I closed the door behind him. I didn't know why Derrick's response was bothering me so much. It wasn't like I wanted to date him. I threw the towel in on dating years ago. After multiple failed attempts at love, I had made a vow. I was going to stay single and embrace being alone for a while. I had my fill of bad relationships with undeserving individuals. I had always been a plus-size woman.

My entire life, I was judged because of my size, so when I was younger, I decided never to do the same to another person. Instead, I would give almost anyone who showed genuine interest in me the opportunity to get to know me. This decision turned out to be an epic failure that resulted in me dating a bunch of terrible people. But that wasn't nearly as bad as when I was boxed into the friend category because "we are just better as friends," only to see the objects of my affection with the universal standard of beauty on their arms. I knew in the end that my size *was* a factor. Too often, I was friend zoned for a size six, and I had finally accepted that fact. I knew I was cute. Too bad the rest of the world didn't think so as well.

I typically ended up dating people I wasn't attracted to. I wasn't even attracted to Derrick. But I never needed to be attracted to his face to get dicked down properly. I knew that since my size twenty-eight body wasn't the ideal body type, I felt it only right never to judge a person on their looks. Even though I put my personal preferences aside, the outcome was the same. I lowered my standards and usually ended up alone, wondering how and why in the hell did I date the lame, to begin with.

After my last failed dating attempt, I knew it was time to give it a rest. All my efforts at love had crashed and burned, but I also watched friends go through hell, all in the name of love. I started to wonder what was the purpose of all of it. Falling in love, getting your heart broken, and doing it all over again just seemed dumb. After all, insanity is repeating the same mistakes and expecting different results, and I was tired of being insane. So I focused on my writing career and things I loved doing. I started traveling, finally getting stamps in my passport. I let my inner geek out and found a love of comic-cons and cosplay. There was nothing better than throwing on a costume and becoming someone else, even if it was just for a little while. Now, I had six novels, three even making it on the Essence bestsellers list, and my dream home. If I needed sex, I had Derrick, and for five years, it was working. Then suddenly, it wasn't anymore.

I turned on my shower, allowing the hot water to steam up the bathroom. Then I pulled my sleep shirt off, dropped it to the floor, and walked into the shower, allowing the hot water to send a jolt of energy through my body. I hated feeling the way I did. I didn't want Derrick, but for some reason, knowing that I was good enough for sex but not good enough for a public date rubbed me the wrong way. And to make things worse, I didn't even enjoy the damn sex. I let the water hit my body, wanting to wash away the night—*and* Derrick.

Chapter 2

I pulled into the dimly lit parking lot of a shabby shopping complex. Three men stood outside the door to the small bar. I never understood why the best open mic spots were always in the middle of the hood. It was unusually warm for a December night. And considering the rain we had been having, it was so warm I expected tornado warnings coming sometime in the next few days.

A knock on my window scared the shit out of me. I saw my friend Morgan standing there with her big goofy grin. Morgan's long, curly hair hung down past her shoulders. I was surprised she didn't have it in her signature ponytail. Morgan was completely black but incredibly light-skinned. And with her curly hair, people often assumed she was biracial, which irritated her to her core.

I opened my car door. "Does your girlfriend only DJ at shitty establishments?" I frowned at her.

"Don't be a bougie bitch tonight, Paige. This entire area is Black-owned and is being revamped to be a dope-ass area." Morgan closed my door behind me.

"And you couldn't invite me *after* the revamping was finished?"

"Shut up, hooker, and come on." Morgan grabbed my arm. I reluctantly trailed along.

I followed her into the building. The good thing about her girlfriend being a DJ was that we never paid to get into her events. Morgan took my hand and led me to the table with some other local poets. The inside was a lot nicer than the outside. Besides the potent mix of weed and incense, the lounge was filled with plush couches, giving it a very comfortable and intimate setting. Large paintings of various artists like Bob Marley, Jimi Hendrix, and Prince hung on the wall. Next to them were little business cards with the artists' names and prices of the paintings printed on them. I noticed a painting of Whitney Houston that I made a mental note to check the price on for my house.

"I'm going to go get a drink." I stopped and turned toward the bar.

"Oh, it's BYOB."

I frowned. "Bitch, why didn't you tell me that before we got here? So you want me to be in this place with no liquor in my system?"

"Don't worry. I brought some Cîroc. Just go get us some setups." Morgan pulled a bottle out of her oversized backpack.

The bartender, an older man, taking more time staring at the women walking in than actually doing his job, handed me two cups, ice, and a Sprite. Suddenly, I felt a tap on my shoulder. I turned around and immediately turned back to the bartender. Standing a few feet away was the band guitarist, Kyra. I felt a warm wave come over my body. I had a tiny girl crush on Kyra, a girl crush that amused Morgan, considering I hadn't dated a woman in over fifteen years. I knew I was the type of bisexual that lesbians weren't particularly fond of. I considered myself a lesbian throughout my twenties, but I met a guy one day and fell head over heels in love with him. After that breakup, I just never dated another woman. But in actuality, I didn't go back to anyone. After enough heartbreak, I took a break and had been single for almost ten years. I just stuck to random sex sessions with guys like Derrick. Kyra was a little taller than me, with these adorable, deep-inset dimples that appeared whenever she smiled or talked. I took a deep breath and glanced back her way. We locked eyes. I typically didn't like colored contacts, but she wore hazel contacts that she rocked very well.

I could almost feel her stepping closer to me. I braced myself, hoping I didn't look crazy. "Is your name Paige?" she asked with an inquisitive expression on her face.

"Um, yes, that's my name." My voice trembled as I responded. My fingertips were tingling. I set the ice down, fearing I might drop the cups.

"I thought so. You don't know me, but I have read a few of your books."

"What?"

"What?" she chuckled. "What? Can a musician not read your books?"

I smiled. "No, I'm sorry. It's just surprising that you even know about my books at all."

Kyra folded her arms. I glanced at how cut her biceps were. Up close, they looked even better than when she was on stage. Kyra had a unique look about her. She always wore baggy cargo pants or jeans with rips at the knees and tees that fit and accentuated her biceps. Her deep sepia-colored skin was blemish free. I always wanted to ask her about her skin care routine. She had thick, naturally curly hair she usually wore in a 'fro or pulled back in a curly Afro puff. Sometimes, she switched it up, wearing some elaborate braided style. Although none of my friends shared the same opinion, they always thought she looked unkempt, or in their words, "dusty," but I found her to be very alluring. They said it was just me being attracted to another artist, but I knew it had to be something more than that. I was drawn to masculine-presenting women primarily, but there was something different about her. She exuded "big dick energy," which was impressive for a woman.

"Yeah, I have a close friend who has all your books. She gave me *Promised Forever*. I was hooked. You are brilliant. I'm still waiting on a follow-up to that book," she declared as she put her left arm on my shoulder. "Seriously, I wanna know what happens to the crew, especially Papi. She was my favorite."

"Wow, you really *have* read it. And yeah, the lesbians are waiting on me to write a sequel. It's coming, I promise." I knew I had to be blushing. I just hoped she didn't notice.

I didn't know what part amazed me more: that she knew my books or that she was talking to me. I tried to concentrate as she gushed over my books. She spoke about the parts she liked the most and what shocked her. The passion she had for my work was intoxicating. I didn't typically enjoy talking about my work, but I could listen to her talk for hours.

"Oh, I love the straight ones too. But I gotta know, are you writing a follow-up for *Crave Me*? That book had me questioning my sexuality for a moment. That scene with Chris and Melisha . . . sheesh." Kyra's bright eyes fixated on me. I wanted her to stop looking at me. I felt she was looking through me.

"There is a follow-up already. It's coming out in a couple of months. I can bring you an early copy at next month's event. And I'm having a book release party, so I can put you on the list if you'd like."

Kyra clapped her hands together. "Don't tease me, woman. Are you for real?"

I nodded my head. "I got you."

"Beautiful and generous. I swear you got a nigga feeling real special right now. I wish it were next month already," Kyra said as her deep dimples appeared. There was something about her smile. It was cute and mischievous, and *very* sexy.

The host called for the musicians to return to the stage to start the night's final set.

"That's my cue to go crush some shit. Until next time, Ms. Paige." Kyra took my hand, pulling it to her mouth and placing a kiss on it. My butterflies were in full flight now.

I smiled as she walked away. As soon as the coast was clear, I grabbed the cups and returned to my friends. I took the bottle and poured myself a shot, taking it back instantly. I needed something to cool the heat radiating from my body, but the burning from the vodka only intensified my craving. I couldn't keep my eyes off Kyra for the rest of the night. She played a solo on her guitar that made the whole room go wild. My heart skipped a beat when she looked directly at me with a sly grin on her face. My body tingled. Either I was having some type of stroke, or this woman was seriously affecting me. I couldn't remember the last time anyone made me feel that way. I wondered if I had ever felt that before in my life.

Morgan was deep in conversation with a poet I wasn't familiar with. I sat on the couch and set her cup near her, placing the ice and my cup on the table. I eavesdropped on their discussion about some New Year's Eve event. I had totally forgotten New Year's Eve was a few days away.

"Oh, my bad." Morgan finally noticed I was there. "Paige, this is Temptress. She's a dope-ass poet. Temptress, this is my homegirl, Paige. She's a writer."

We shook hands. Temptress was the epitome of the plus-size woman I wanted to be. Shaped like an hourglass, she was all hips and had ass for days. Her waist was snatched, accentuated by a belt with a giant sun as the belt buckle. Her black bodysuit looked like it was painted on her. I was in awe and slightly envious. My stomach wouldn't let me be great like that. My stomach would show regardless, even with the best shapewear and waist trainers.

"Oh, what do you write?" Temptress focused her attention on me.

"Books, novels."

"Oh really? That's dope. I want to put out a book of poetry. Maybe we can talk later."

"Sure, just add me on Facebook and shoot me a DM," I smiled.

My eyes caught a glimpse of Kyra putting on her guitar. Then the band started to warm up, and people started sitting down, knowing the show was about to begin.

"I'll get your info after the show. Morgan, let's finish talking later." Temptress sashayed back to her table.

My eyes focused on Kyra. Morgan immediately noticed and nudged me. She giggled. "Lord, are you still crushing on her?"

"No," I lied. "Leave me alone."

"It's cute. I know you will come back to our side one of these days." Morgan crossed her arms.

"Shut up, and I never left your side. I just also enjoy the other side too."

Morgan's lip curled. "Riiiighhhttt."

The band started their cover of "The Way" by Jill Scott. I couldn't take my eyes off Kyra. She was having some kind of effect on me. Maybe I missed the lady pond more than I knew.

Chapter 3

New Year's Eve wasn't a festive time for me. While others were planning big nights of parties and romance, I had a night of writing, Netflix, and pizza ahead of me. I was doing exactly what I wanted to do for the new year. I was going to spend it by myself, writing—the same thing I had done for the last six years. They say that who you kiss at midnight is who you will be with in the upcoming year. I was hoping that one of these years, sitting home writing at midnight would turn me into a New York Times Bestselling author.

After more than one unsuccessful intervention, my friends had finally given up hope of me finding love or getting me out of the house on N.Y.E. They didn't believe I would stick to my lone wolf status, but after six years, they realized I was in it for the long haul. So I settled in on my oversized couch with my Doritos and wine and prepared to write while flipping back and forth between various channels' New Year's Eve coverage. I would focus on writing until the clock struck midnight; then I would put in an old classic movie and watch it until

I fell asleep. My New Year's resolutions were set. I would write something compelling and spend the year working on my career. I made a decision, and I planned on sticking to it.

I had been thinking about my night with Derrick. I realized that even my lone wolf was craving a little more than just random sex. Could I possibly want to try a relationship again? Could the detail missing from Derrick possibly be that I just didn't want casual sex anymore? The idea of dating and relationships made me cringe. I had vowed to stay away from heartbreak, but now, it seemed my heart might be calling for another shot at the real thing. Could I possibly have a mix of both worlds, not a full relationship, but something more than just a casual romp in the bed? I wanted to find a happy middle ground, someone who could offer a little companionship from time to time without requiring too much of my time.

I discussed the situation with Morgan while at the lounge the other night. She believed that finally, after all these years of being alone, it was time for me to be open to dating. I found dating exhausting. I hated dating apps. I typically only matched with losers or guys wanting to fetishize my body. But meeting in person never worked either. I was never the one people noticed. And the few who had attempted to talk to me seemed to be more interested in the author than me as a person.

I took another small break from writing to make a list of what I wanted in a companion. I knew the most important thing was I would not allow myself to end up head over heels in love with someone, but I would at least be open to going on a few dates here and there. And to even consider dating, I would not date a person unless they knocked me off my feet in the first moments of meeting. I would not take the time to get to know anyone I didn't feel a mental and physical attraction toward. And I would not date any closed- or narrow-minded individuals who didn't share similar interests with me. They must be able to make me laugh and be able to hold intelligent conversations with me. They would have to be as driven or more driven than I am and have goals they wanted to accomplish. I added a few ridiculous details to my list, like, must have geeky ways, must be able to know what movie I randomly say lines from, and must love shows like *Spartacus, Game of Thrones,* and *Harry Potter.* I was happy with my list, for I knew this type of person didn't exist. I would probably be a lone wolf for life by keeping my list. I realized I was being ridiculous, but I didn't care.

The bipolar weather was still warm. It felt more like spring than winter, which almost made me consider going to the event Morgan and Temptress were at. But I had a plan, and I was sticking to it. This was my first year in my new house, and I was happy in my *Fortress of Solitude.*

Before long, I was deep into the zone, writing a scene I could only hope would make my fans crave more. Midchapter, my mind began to wonder what was happening outside of my house. I flipped from Microsoft Word to Facebook in my internet browser. It was filled with the usual NYE photos of people showing off their outfits, liquor stashes, and talking about going to church. I decided to post a message on my wall.

Spending my night writing. Happy NYE, everyone.

I turned on my Spotify playlist filled with random songs I loved to use as inspiration and clicked back to my document. I instantly regretted my decision to scroll because it took me out of my zone. I needed liquid libations to get back into my writing flow, and I was out of wine. So I got up, walked into my kitchen, and pulled out a bottle of Moscato someone had given me as a gift. I popped the cork and poured a glass, taking the glass and bottle back to my living room, where I got comfortable again and returned to my computer. Then something flashing behind the top of my document caught my attention. I clicked back over to my internet browser and paused when I saw I had a new message from Kyra Preston.

My bottom lip fell open. Why was my girl crush contacting me?

I could admit I had a few celebrity girl crushes. Tessa Thompson, Michelle Rodriguez, and Lena

Waithe were just a few. Unlike the celebrities, Kyra was my only crush close to home, but she was equally unobtainable to me. She oozed sex appeal. I believed it was a mixture of how she played the guitar and her arms. I always had a thing for nice arms, and her biceps looked like she never missed arm day in the gym. Plus, Kyra played her guitar with an intensity that rivaled any of the greats. There was a deep soul in her sexy.

I snapped back to reality to see I wasn't dreaming. Her name was sitting there on the chat list. I took a few minutes to stare at her name before clicking on her chat bubble.

Finally, I opened the message.

Kyra: You should write about a musician known for her smooth transitions on her strings and romantic exploits.

I smiled. I found her message really cute, so I typed a quick response.

Paige: Oh really?

I hit my forehead. I wrote novels for a living, and all I could think to say was, "oh really"? Then the three little dots instantly appeared, alerting me that she was responding.

Kyra: Yep. But that's just my narcissism speaking. So what are you writing about, if you don't mind me asking?

She was making small talk. I had to do better than last time. I took a sip of wine and began to type.

Paige: Right now, it's a story about a girl who has sworn off dating, but her friends continue to try to change her mind. Just trying to pull a little from reality.

Kyra: Reality? I mean, I hear reality makes for the best writing. But I don't see how that could be your reality at all. But if you want, feel free to add an enigmatic musician who loves music but has a secret love of the written word. Oh, and is known for her sexual exploits.

Sexual exploits? I was intrigued. I wasn't the best at knowing when someone was flirting with me. But I felt like that might have been a flirt.

Paige: Hmm, interesting. I will consider that.

Kyra: The musician could offer to read the woman's work, but they struggle to be in the same room due to the all-out sexual tension.

It was as if someone knocked the wind out of me. I had been out of the game for a while, but that was *definitely* a flirt. I read the message again. And then again, because I knew I had to be tripping. There was no way she was *really* flirting with me. I didn't know how to respond. I decided to take the easy way out.

Paige: LMAO.

I sent two Facebook gifs of animals laughing hard. Immediately, the writing dots appeared again.

Kyra: Damn, that's a lot of laughing. It wasn't that funny. I'm sexy.

I didn't know if it was the wine or what, but I decided to take a little chance.

Paige: I didn't say you weren't.

I waited for a response. There was a pause before a gif appeared of a dog smirking with sunglasses on. I couldn't help but laugh.

The conversation continued. I found myself laughing at her silliness. She was very intelligent. She didn't use broken text lingo that I loathed, even in messaging. She let me know that she had the night off, which was rare considering the band she was in was one of the most popular in Memphis. Kyra asked a lot of questions about my writing. Suddenly, the excitement started to wear off. It was beginning to feel like just another writer trying to pick my brain about publishing. I shrugged my shoulders and prepared to answer the way I always did. If she did ask me about publishing a book, I already knew I would tell her that I wasn't allowed to read unsolicited materials and give her a link to some information about publishing on Amazon. I was all prepared to be disappointed, but she hit me differently.

Kyra: As much as I love this picture I have in my brain of your signature smile staring at my boring texts, I have to ask. Why aren't you going out tonight?

I thought about the question for a moment.

Paige: I like my fortress of solitude, and I have no life.

Kyra: I refuse to believe that. You might like to say you have no life, but I have a feeling you live on a mental plane that does not allow you to comfortably participate in the so-called lives that the mere mortals around you engage in. Or maybe you are afraid to step out and do the things you really want to do. Either way, I know you are way too full of life not to have one.

I suddenly felt uncomfortable. How could she read me so well? Was I *that* transparent? The truth was I did feel out of place in regular social settings like bars and clubs. However, I felt the most comfortable in my costumes at Comic-Con, where I spent most of the time being someone else.

Paige: Are you staring in my window or something? How can you know me so well?

Kyra: They say great minds think alike. I am totally an introverted extrovert. I am comfortable only when I am playing. But most of the time, I want to come home to my empty house and not leave it.

A calmness swept over my body. Finally, someone I barely knew made me feel more comfortable via Facebook messaging than any of my friends had done in months. I felt like I could pour out my soul to her.

Paige: You are so right. My friends give me a hard time because I love being alone in my home. One, I just recently purchased my house, and I enjoy being in it, but they think I need someone. It gets annoying.

I watched as the writing dots moved for a few moments. I felt excited *and* anxious. I wanted to know what her reply was going to be.

Kyra: Your friends probably think they have your best interest in mind. I get it. You are intelligent, professional, and sexy as hell. Therefore, you should allow someone to enjoy the pleasure of such beautiful company.

Sexy as hell? I felt a heat filling my cheeks. Usually, words like cute, sweet, nice, and talented were used to describe me. The only person who had ever called me sexy as hell was Derrick, and he didn't count because it was to get in my pants the first time. I didn't know how to respond. A piece of me wanted to say thank you. I mean, shouldn't I thank a person for such a compliment? But a larger, more dominant part of me felt cautious. Was she playing a sick joke on me? No one ever called me sexy. Was this a plot to get close to the author in hopes of getting something out of me?

On top of my paranoia, I was also stuck in a state of utter confusion. Why was I so excited over her? I know it had been a long time since I had dated anyone, but damn, I shouldn't be acting so thirsty over a couple of DMs.

I suddenly didn't want to continue talking. She was getting a little too close for comfort, and I felt my brain shutting down with each passing moment. I didn't want to come off as a dork. I knew I needed to end the conversation.

Paige: Well, it's almost midnight. I'm sure you have better things to do than chat with me.

Kyra: Aw, man, trying to get rid of me already?

Paige: LOL, no. I just know if I continue chatting with you, I might not want to stop.

I instantly regretted pressing send. I just overtly flirted with a woman. I sat at the edge of my chair, wondering what her response would be. Wineglass in hand, I watched those little writing dots move much slower than usual. Obviously, I said too much. I wanted to slap myself for coming off so eager. I instantly thought of tons of alternative responses that were so much better than the one I gave. My heart almost fell out of my chest when a text box appeared.

Kyra: Who said I wanted you to stop? Lay it on me, Paige. I welcome any and everything you want to throw my way.

I couldn't stop smiling. I knew I should tell her I was straight, but something stopped me. I was enjoying the moment and wasn't ready to end it soon.

Chapter 4

I didn't remember when or how I got into bed. As my eyes adjusted to the noonday sun filling my room, the night came back to my mind. It had to be a dream. I wondered if it was all a dream. Did I drink a little too much and let my personal, lustful flights of fancy get the best of me, filling my dreams with wild, realistic fantasies of the guitar player?

I ran my hand under my pillow until finally touching my cell phone. I picked it up and opened my Facebook Messenger app. It was flooded with "Happy New Year" messages from friends and fans of my work. I scrolled through the enormous numbers of messages until my finger stopped on a name. There it was. Kyra's direct message. It wasn't a dream after all.

I scrolled to the beginning of our messaging and began to reread the entire thread. I wanted to analyze each word and emoji, ensuring I didn't miss anything. I smiled, laughing out loud at numerous parts of the conversation. I cringed at my awkward moments. I needed to get better at flirting. My dork side definitely showed up during the conversation. Even staring at the evidence, it felt surreal. These types of things didn't happen to me. Gorgeous musicians looked at my friends, not the shy and awkward big girl who usually held the purses while her friends mingled.

I didn't want to get out of bed. I wanted to lie there and live in the previous night's moments. I brought the New Year in chatting with a woman who, until now, always felt like a beautiful fantasy. Now, with a direct message on Facebook, she had become real.

I had the day off. I suddenly didn't feel like spending the day listening to music and writing. I wanted to get out. So I called Morgan and asked her to meet me at one of our favorite local dining places for lunch.

I got out of bed with a pep in my step. I was floating. I could feel it. I took a longer-than-normal shower, dried off, and covered myself in one of my favorite Bath and Body Works fragrance lotions. I sprayed the matching mist on my body before brushing my long hair. Then I pulled my long hair into a neat ponytail and wore a headband to cover my slightly curly edges. After that, I picked up my ChapStick and paused. I didn't want to wear ChapStick, so I pulled out a red gloss and covered my lips. I even switched up from my usual jeans and T-shirts to go for a pair of distressed skinny jeans and a flouncy blouse I had gotten from Torrid months ago but never worn.

I arrived at the Side Street Grill to find Morgan nursing her first cocktail. Side Street was considered an honorary gay establishment, even though it wasn't gay at all. Over the years, the small house turned into a cigar bar and restaurant and had become the place people hung out, drank, and chilled.

Morgan's hair was pulled tightly back in a ponytail, with her long, curly hair falling down her back. Although completely African American, her very light skin and curls made people constantly question her ethnicity. I walked over with a large smile on my face. She stared at me with a curious look.

"What's this?" she questioned, waving her finger up and down at me.

I sat down without saying anything. The waitress walked over and took my drink order.

"I don't know what you are talking about," I smirked.

"Whatever, hooker, You come in here with a Cheshire-cat grin on your face, and you think you aren't going to tell me? You got on lip gloss and fitted jeans and no graphic tee. Yeah, something's up. What the hell is going on with you?"

I couldn't stop smiling. I pulled my phone out and scrolled to the message. Holding the phone tightly to my chest, I turned and looked Morgan in her eyes.

"Something strange happened to me last night. I think I might be having some type of psychotic episode or something," I whispered.

"What in the hell are you talking about?" Morgan stared at me with her drink in hand.

"I'm going to show you something, but you have to promise not to freak out." I didn't take my eyes off my friend, who didn't seem like she was taking me seriously.

"Bitch, if you don't say it already." Morgan threw her hands up in frustration.

I pulled my hands from my chest and handed her the phone. Morgan looked at the message. Within seconds, I felt a punch to my shoulder.

"Shut up! Kyra? *Really?* What in the hell? What is this? I'm so confused, " Morgan squealed as she continued to read the message exchange.

"I know. She just randomly hit me up, and we started chatting."

"Girl, there is some serious flirting going on here," Morgan said without looking up from my phone. "On both sides. Paige, you are flirting on here." Her outburst caused a few people to look in our direction. We both lowered our heads in embarrassment.

"I told you I'm having some type of breakdown. I don't flirt with people. And it's Kyra."

"Oh Lord, she's flirting with this damn woman. I caught yo' ass staring at her at the last poetry night, looking like a lovesick puppy dog." Morgan grinned. "This is so weird. I mean, it's dope. I don't know much about her outside of the poetry scene, but she's always been cool people."

"Morgan, I don't know what it is. I haven't felt this way in . . . ever. Even with my exes, they didn't make me feel the way I felt conversing with her last night. I felt like I'd known Kyra for years. It was organic and refreshing."

"That's awesome." Morgan's voice went an octave higher. "That's always the best when you can just vibe with someone. I mean, yeah, it's weird that you are flirting with a woman."

"Why? I am bi, Morgan."

"Eh," Morgan winced. "I pretty much consider you straight with a little curve at the most."

"Oh, shut up." We both laughed.

"Sorry, I mean, it's been forever since you mentioned a woman. I just figured we lost you to the world of the dicks."

I threw my napkin at her. "It's not that. I just haven't met anyone who I like. I can never find anyone who I can have a genuinely cool conversation with. This was different. I don't think I've ever meshed so well with someone off the bat like this."

The waitress arrived with my drink. I quickly took a big sip of the fruity libation. I was on cloud nine from just one conversation. But that feeling soon faded. I realized it was one conversation. What if she never contacted me again? My smile faded. Morgan noticed instantly.

"Uh-oh, what's that face for?" she questioned.

"Morgan, this is ridiculous. I shouldn't be giddy like this after one conversation. Hell, she might not ever contact me again. I'm insane, or maybe I have some type of illness. Do I have a fever?" I patted my head and neck to check if I was hot.

"Fever, yeah, looks like you got that gay fever that's been going around. Probably from watching too much TV or something." Morgan sipped her drink. I threw my middle finger up at her.

"Nah, I'm blaming you. Hanging out with a mega-lesbo like you has to rub off on me. I need some straight friends." I motioned like I was wiping something off my shirt.

Morgan playfully hit my hand. "Ha-ha, funny. But seriously, Paige, you *are* tripping. You've been single for longer than I can remember. I'm happy someone has you a little giddy, though."

"And I guess it being a woman doesn't hurt." I took another sip of my water.

Morgan smirked. "Listen, at this point, I'm totally down with anyone who can make you even consider leaving that *lone wolf* bullshit behind.

You deserve to be happy, and by the way, you are smiling. Kyra might be that person," she reassured me.

Morgan made me feel a little better, but I was still stuck in my own thoughts. I stared at the message on my phone. I wondered what she was doing. Would it seem desperate of me to text her first? Finally, I decided I had to put it out of my mind. No matter how wonderful the conversation, I wasn't going to let a few passing moments of bliss completely distort what I knew to be reality. Things like this didn't happen . . . well, not to me.

Morgan and I chatted about various topics while waiting on our food to arrive. A few people we knew in passing would come up and make small talk before going to their respective tables. I tried to concentrate on what they were saying, but my mind was elsewhere. I felt like a junkie eager for her next hit. Every time I heard the chime of my messenger notification, my heart stopped. I was relieved when our food finally arrived. At least eating gave me something to do with my idle hands.

"You know you *could* send her a message," Morgan said without looking up from her plate.

"You think?"

"Why not? She made the first move. I don't see anything wrong with you making the second one," she said while munching on a french fry covered in way too much ketchup. I could never understand Morgan's addiction to ketchup.

But I knew she was right. I *could* make the first move, but I knew it had to be a calculated one. I didn't want to come off corny or anxious. I wanted to be smooth and alluring. I picked up my phone and opened the messenger app, staring at the typing box. I had nothing.

"What are you waiting for?" Morgan questioned.

"I literally cannot think of a single thing to say."

"Bitch, you write books for a living. Ugh, you are hopeless." She shook her head as she took my phone from me. Then she began typing something. I heard a faint click when she pressed send. My heart was racing.

"What did you say?" I panicked as I grabbed the phone from her and read the message.

Paige: Happy New Year.

I looked at Morgan and the goofy smile on her face. I wanted to smack her. She was a poet. She could have easily come up with a plethora of catchy sayings. But instead, she sent a generic message I was more than sure Kyra had seen as many times that day as I had.

Suddenly, my messenger notification chimed, causing me to almost jump out of my seat. I looked at the locked screen on my phone. It was from her. I quickly unlocked my phone and read the message.

Kyra: Happy New year, sweetheart. How did you sleep?

I knew my face had to be beet red from the heat on my cheeks.

Paige: Great, better than usual. I blame the wine.

Kyra: The right one will do it to you every time. Sucks, though. I was hoping my entertaining wit had something to do with it.

I bit my lip. I wanted to say the right thing. Not come off as thirsty, but funny and cool.

Paige: You were a'ight.

I added a wink emoji and one with sunglasses.

Kyra: Ouch.

Paige: :)

Kyra: Cute.

I bit my bottom lip again. She had me giddy. I couldn't remember the last time I was giddy over anyone. I wanted more. I wanted to see what would happen if we talked in person.

Paige: So, what does your day look like?

Kyra: Well, I'm going on a short tour. I'll be out of the city for about a month.

Fuck. I didn't like hearing that, but then again, that would give me time to get to know her. The last thing I needed to do was be around her right then. I was in unfamiliar territory and didn't know if I could come out unscathed.

I wasn't sure how to respond. I had been out of the dating game for almost seven years. So I didn't know what the proper protocols for flirting were. I wanted to play it cool. The problem was that I had no idea how to play anything cool. I was the epitome of a dork with minimal experience in try-

ing to date. I felt my blood pressure rising. I took
a deep breath. I was going to give myself a panic
attack, and I didn't know if this girl was genuinely
interested in me. Men were so much easier than
women for me.

Kyra: Damn, did I lose you already?

Shit. I was so consumed in my thoughts that I
completely forgot to message her again. I quickly
typed.

Paige: No, sorry. Out eating with my friend
Morgan. I think you guys know each other.

Kyra: Hell yeah, I know her light-bright ass. Tell
her I said what's up. Where are you eating? I bet
it's good.

Paige: Side Street.

Kyra: Oh, y'all out trying to meet some women?

Paige: What? LOL.

Kyra: The only reason lesbians go to Side
Street is to meet chicks.

Paige: And the food and drinks are good.

Kyra: True. You just enjoy the food and not the
environment, all right? I ain't trying to lose your
attention yet.

I blushed. Morgan couldn't help but laugh as
she finished off her ketchup fries. I contemplated
what my next line would be. I ate a couple of fries
while thinking of my response. Then it hit me.
Kyra obviously thought I was gay. Would she have
an issue with me being bisexual? I decided to cross

that bridge when I got to it. For now, I was just going to enjoy the conversation.

Paige: LOL. I'll remember that. And yes, the food is good. Not as good as my food, though.

I grinned as I watched the response dots moving.

Kyra: Oh word. I can't wait to find out. And yes, I just invited myself to partake in your culinary cuisine. I'm a fat girl at heart. So don't mention food and not expect to feed me.

Paige: Anytime.

I felt proud of my budding flirting skills. I started to finish my food while listening to Morgan's recent relationship issues. I cringed, quickly remembering why I chose to be a lone wolf in the first place. There wasn't a couple more perfect for each other than Morgan and Sybil. If they were having issues, then I knew relationships were fucked. I suddenly didn't want to flirt anymore. I didn't want to like anyone, especially not a hot lady guitarist. That was a recipe for disaster. There was no way she wasn't a whore. If she had this effect on me, I knew many other women were going through the same thing. I decided there was no way this could be anything serious to her.

Doubt crept into my mind. She read my books, and she did ask a lot of questions about my publishing. Was this just another person trying to cozy up to me in hopes of getting on? So many people thought being a writer made me rich. I was very comfortable. Hitting Essence bestsellers with my last four books, I was able to purchase my house. But I still worked a nine to five. Writing provided me with enough money to travel as much as I wanted and live very comfortably. Was this just an attempt to use me or get something out of me? It wouldn't be the first time. I knew that story all too well, and it seemed to be the more plausible option at the moment. I shifted my body in my seat.

"What's wrong with you?" Morgan asked, noticing my sullen expression.

"Why is she flirting with me? Is she another Rachel or Donna?"

I thought about the last two women I talked to. Both were fans of my work and romanticized the author. But once knowing nerdy girl was the pen, they quickly lost interest in anything besides wanting to travel with me or live off me. Kyra loved my work, but was she going to be like them?

Morgan took my phone out of my hand.

"See, this is your problem. Every time someone attempts to be nice, you find a reason to run. Remember when that dude from the bowling alley offered to buy you a drink? You called him weird because he was wearing a Marvel T-shirt."

"No, I said he was weird because he was wearing a Marvel T-shirt *and* said he didn't watch any of the movies or read any of the comics. So why wear a shirt and know nothing about what you're wearing?"

Morgan frowned. "Girl, get a grip. Now, understand I'm *not* saying jump headfirst. She is a musician, after all. But there is nothing wrong with testing the waters. Maybe there is more there than you know. Only one way to find out."

"You are way too eager for me to hop back into the dating pond. Let us not forget Donna." I tightened my eyes at Morgan. She laughed.

"Girl," Morgan sighed, "first off, Donna was like twenty years ago."

"It was only like twelve years." I frowned at her statement. I wasn't that bad.

"Second off, fuck Donna. She was the worst. And we aren't talking about her. We are talking about *you* jumping back into the dating pool. Man, woman—at this point, I truly don't care. Just get out here and have some fun." Morgan smirked as she sipped her drink.

I nodded. "I guess you're right. I'm over here acting like the woman asked me to marry her. I don't even really know her. So, she has incredible conversation and stuff. But that doesn't make her the one. I'm trippin'."

"Exactly. Take it one day at a time. Listen to her words *and* her actions," Morgan reassured me. "Oh, but one thing about Donna. Don't do that again."

"What?"

"Allow a bad experience to cut off the possibility of love in your life."

We looked at each other, Morgan with a serious expression I don't see on her face that often. I knew she was right. Even with the men I've seen, I never dated anyone seriously. I made my vow, and I stuck to it. But now, maybe it was time to change my vow.

The waitress walked over and took our empty plates. I realized Kyra hadn't responded to my last message. I shook the thoughts out of my head. I wasn't going to give her unnecessary power. Then just as I went to put my phone in my bag, the messenger notification rang.

Kyra: Sorry about the delay. Trying to get packed. I will take you up on that the moment I get back. Until then, I will have to devour your intellect to feed my hunger.

Damn, she's good.

Chapter 5

The time had come, and I was a nervous wreck. Kyra was back in town. I knew it was only a matter of time before we spent time together. We chatted nonstop throughout the entire month. I woke up every morning with a message from her, usually something she sent in the wee hours of the morning when she was getting in from her different gigs. I wondered when she slept because she always seemed to respond to my messages almost as soon as I sent them. If she was going to be away on stage, she always told me so I would know she wouldn't be able to respond right away. That was one thing I liked about her. I hated when people didn't respond to messages.

The monthly artist lounge was Sunday, and she would be playing there. So when Kyra told me she was looking forward to seeing me, I knew I wanted to look special.

"Bitch, you gon' let me dress you or what?" my boisterous coworker and friend, Tara, blurted out.

"I think I can dress myself," I replied as I finished typing notes on my last customer.

I was lucky enough to work in a call center where I genuinely loved my coworkers. So I listened to my friend and coworker to my right, Shantel, finishing her call. I was always amazed by how fast she talked.

"In what world? All you wear is jeans and T-shirts." Tara said as she frowned. "You going to see this gir . . . dude for the first time, so you need to be beat to the gods." Tara caught herself. Tara was out and proud at work. She was straight until she met her wife, Lauren. They married and now had two kids, a beautiful house, and a dog. She was the epitome of the lesbian dream. Although she knew I was bisexual, I wasn't overly open at work. Not out of shame, I just didn't want to be another topic of conversation in the call center. One thing about call centers is they were all messy as fuck, no matter where you are. So, for now, Kyra was simply known as the gender-neutral "Kay."

I was working toward writing full time, but for now, my nine-to-five paid way too much for me to give it up so easily. I worked in sales for a national insurance company. Although office politics were annoying, the commission checks for doing hardly any work made it the perfect fit. I also had a set Monday through Friday schedule with no weekends. Plus, I had been there so long I knew all the ins and outs of working the system. I had FMLA set for days I needed or wanted off. I was able to do everything I needed to do. Plus, I could talk to my coworkers, who I genuinely liked, and also get some writing done while at work. It was a good gig. I figured I'd stay there until my writing led to bigger and better opportunities.

"I agree, Paige," Shantel, my cubicle neighbor, joined the conversation by turning her chair around. Her long body wave lace front bounced with every head movement. I was convinced she spent half of her commission check on her hair and nails. They always looked perfect. I tried lace fronts but got irritated by not being able to touch my scalp. No matter how much I wanted to be, I wasn't the weave girl. During her last call, Shantel had completely changed the makeup she was wearing from a natural look to a deep smoky eye. I knew it would change again before the day was over.

"You gotta do more than some jeans and a T-shirt."

"OK," I replied. "How about jeans and a super cute blouse? Distressed jeans, show a little skin?" I smiled.

They grimaced at my comment.

"Seriously, Paige," Shantel put her hand on my knee. "You really seem to like this guy. There is nothing wrong with showing him that you have more than one side to you. Show him that you can be both sexy *and* simple."

"Simple?" I frowned.

"That's what I'm saying," Tara said as she threw her hands up. "Girl, you want him to know steak is cooking, so you gotta let him hear it sizzle." She shook her shimmy, causing us all to laugh.

I knew they were right. Kyra was already familiar with my plain-Jane look. My jeans and graphic tee game were on point. But I needed to show her something else.

"OK, we can go to Torrid and try to find something. But I'm telling you now, I'm not wearing any heels or no super tight shit." I pointed at Tara, already thoroughly familiar with how she would try to dress me if I let her. Tara was also a big woman, but unlike me, she had no issues wearing anything she wanted. She proudly flaunted her stomach in spandex bodycon dresses and crop tops.

"Ugh, you suck. Good thing it's cold as shit outside. You get away with what I would normally try to put you in. Oh shit." Tara sat down. She immediately went into professional mode, returning to the customer she had put on hold minutes ago. "OK, I'm so sorry about that wait, but it looks like I found the issue."

Shantel and I both shook our heads at Tara before turning back around. I didn't know why I even told them about the situation. I knew they would get too excited. Tara had already attempted to set me up with every eligible man and woman she knew. She was convinced I needed to find a person to marry so I could be like her and her wife. She refused to believe I was happy being single. Shantel was younger than us but was married with a son. They had one of those relationships where they spent every moment together, even spending every break on the phone with each other. Although Tara had no problems going out, we could never get Shantel to go anywhere. I respected that she and her husband truly loved being together all the time. I just didn't understand it.

Tara and I headed to Torrid after work. To our surprise, Shantel met us up there when she got off. I sat on a bench while they scoured the racks for what they thought would be the perfect look. I vetoed the first few options. No, I wasn't wearing my arms out; no, I wasn't wearing anything short, even if wearing tights. Finally, Shantel noticed a cute black sweater with a keyhole cut out at the chest. I tried it on with a pair of soft denim jeans. Tara insisted on a new push-up bra, which, I couldn't lie, made my cleavage look amazing through the tiny keyhole.

I promised Tara I would let her do my hair and makeup on Sunday. Her side hustle was hair, and she was great at it. I knew from our discussions that Kyra wasn't a fan of makeup or weave. She complimented me on my hair and let me know she would love to see me wear my natural curl pattern instead of always flat ironing my locs. So I made sure Tara understood that I was to have soft makeup. She complained the entire time. She wanted me in full glam with big eyelashes. That wasn't what this was, and although I had to stress it to her, I knew she would do it, even if she complained the entire time.

Kyra had already blown my mind with each day that passed. I was surprised by how attentive she was. She paid attention to everything I said, even the small things. Kyra complimented more than just my personality and smile. She told me that she loved big women and joked about how she used to be a fat girl. She had a love affair with music and food. Whenever either subject came up, she got excited like a kid in a candy store. We could talk for hours, and it felt like minutes. I couldn't remember the last time that happened.

I was worn out by the time I made it home. I dropped my bags on my living room floor and sat in my oversized chair, where I propped up my feet on my ottoman and picked up my house phone to call my best friend, Mina. Mina was a nurse who traveled to different states on travel nurse contracts. I would see her a few times a year when she

would take a break between assignments or when I
decided to visit her in whatever city she was in. She
was currently on assignment in St. Thomas. I en-
vied her and her surroundings.

I pressed the talk button only to hear the indica-
tion that I had messages. So I dialed into my house
phone's voicemail. I had one message.

"Paige, it's Mark. Give me a call." Mark, my
publisher, sounded rushed as usual.

I dialed his number, and he picked up on the
second ring.

"Paige," he sighed, "where have you been, boo?"

Mark was a bestselling author-turned-publisher.
His small book imprint had grown to become the
world's largest urban literary publishing company.

"Nowhere, just working. What's going on?" I put
my feet back on the ground.

"I've emailed you with no responses. How are
you feeling with the upcoming release?" he questioned.

I covered my mouth. I hadn't checked my author email in weeks.

"Man, I'm sorry. I have been swamped at work.
Trying to do a lot of overtime. I feel good. My local
release party is coming along great. Think you can
make the trip?"

"I don't think I can. Seems we might be taking
the company to Hollywood a little sooner than we
expected. Got some options lining up."

I tried to remain calm. "Oh, that sounds great, Mark." I loved writing books, but I wanted to write for film and TV more than anything. I knew the company was trying to make the switch to Hollywood and only hoped I would be along for the ride.

"Yeah, so enjoy the release, and if things work how I think they will, maybe you will be quitting that job that keeps getting in the way of you writing books. And while we are on the subject, when am I getting the next book synopsis?"

"Hey, so, I have an idea. How would you feel about me maybe writing a lesbian erotic novel?"

He was silent on the phone for a few minutes. I listened as Mark asked someone to open the numbers from the anthology I was a part of. He muttered something that I couldn't understand.

"Don't get me wrong; your lesbian book was fantastic, but it also was your slowest seller. They just don't buy the books the way your regular audience does, and I'm not sure I want you alienating your audience."

That was disappointing, but I knew he was right. "That makes sense," I agreed. The last thing I wanted to do was alienate my fans, who had supported me over the years.

"All right, I know you have the release coming up, but get me a synopsis soon for a new book. We gotta keep them coming, and hopefully, finally, get you on that New York Times list." His usual, rushed voice was back.

"I got it."

I wanted to throw the phone across the room. I hung up and screamed. I felt ashamed. I was living on this cloud, completely ignoring my responsibilities. I grabbed my computer to check my email. He was right. They had sent me multiple emails about everything from my upcoming release and asking about a new book. I didn't have a synopsis or an idea written down at all. Now, I had a weekend to figure it out, and I was supposed to see Kyra on Sunday.

I wondered if my book didn't sell well because it was about lesbians or because it was a book about lesbians from a perceived straight woman. Would openly stating that I was bisexual alienate both sides? I knew lesbians typically held disdain for bisexual women. I'd been a part of many debates with lesbians about bisexual women. The overwhelming thought about bisexual women was that they were greedy or not able to make up their minds on what they really wanted. What would Kyra think if I told her that I identified as bi or that the last person I was with was a man, even if it was years ago?

Kyra was a stud. She radiated masculine energy, and it was sexy as fuck to me. But I knew studs were tough on bisexual women, which I found funny since many of my stud friends enjoyed sleeping with straight women. So would Kyra end things with me if she knew the truth? Would that be the end of us before we ever really got started?

Suddenly, I realized how silly I sounded. I was forming a whole relationship with a woman I hadn't spent more than a few moments with. True, we had spent the last month tied to our phones, but that didn't make for a relationship. I didn't know if Kyra would look at me as just another flip-flopping bi chick. I didn't know if that would be a concern at all.

I wanted more than anything to continue to get to know Kyra and explore where this was heading. In only one month, she had opened me up and made me think that maybe a relationship wouldn't be the worst thing on earth.

How quickly the tides could change. I went from a bona fide lone wolf to giddy over the possibility of a relationship. Was this fate? Out of all the people in the universe, why did she come into my life when she did? Kyra was a remarkable woman, and everything in my soul wanted to know what would happen next. But I knew this wasn't normal. Outside of Derrick, I mostly ignored advances from men. And even with Derrick, it was strictly a sexual relationship. But I desired Kyra more than I had ever wanted anyone in my life. So why was the universe playing this cruel trick on me? I didn't want to fall in love again, but I found myself standing at the edge of a cliff, inches from falling.

Suddenly, my house phone rang, startling me out of my daydream. I had to stop this. I was daydreaming way too much.

"Hello," I said without checking the caller ID.

"What's wrong with you?" my best friend Mina said drily.

"Nothing, well. I just got off the phone with my publisher. He already wants a new book." I slumped down in my chair.

"Well, better get to writing," she replied with no energy. I knew she had to be tired. She worked twelve-hour shifts, so our communication hadn't been much lately. "So, besides that, what else is going on? Still trying to see that girl?"

"Why she gotta be 'that girl'? Ugh," I laughed.

Mina grunted. "I don't want to sound negative because I know you enjoy this. Of course, I want you to be happy, but I don't know. I just don't get a good feeling when I think about her."

"You don't know her, Mina. You've only seen two photos I sent you."

"I know, which is why I'm trying to let you have it. Maybe it's just my Cancer Spidey-sense, but I just don't get a good feeling at all," she grumbled.

I couldn't help but roll my eyes. Mina never liked anyone I dated but with good reason. She was never afraid to let me know that I had horrible taste in people and that I tended to accept whatever someone gave me. She was tired of me giving so much energy to people she deemed not to be on my level. Unlike my coworker, Tara, who felt that I should give anyone a chance who was interested in me, Mina believed I should wait until someone worthy of me came along. After my last relationship, I agreed with her, leading to my long relationship hiatus.

"Mina, Kyra is nice. But I think I've found a new friend even if we don't end up together." I placed my phone back on my ottoman.

"Girl, one of these days, you are going to listen to me," she sighed. "You gon' stop being quick to call people 'friend.'"

I rolled my eyes again. I loved my friend, but she tended to be very negative when it came to anyone trying to be in my life. Of course, I couldn't lie and say she wasn't right most of the time, but for once, I wanted her at least to start with a positive attitude.

"I'm not trying to be hard on you. I'm sure she's a cool chick. I just don't like that you are so excited so quickly. Your nose is wide open, and you have not spent any time with her. Just pump your brakes a little bit and truly get to know her. Treat it like poker. Put your game face on, and don't let her know what cards you're holding."

She was right. I had been burned so many times in the past. And it never failed. . . . Whenever someone broke my heart, they would reappear for a second chance or try to be my friend. And I always allowed my exes to be friends with me. None of my buddies could understand how I could be friends with people who mistreated me. I couldn't explain it myself.

I knew Mina only wanted what was best for me, but I just wasn't in the mind-set to hear it. So I used the excuse of needing to write to get off the phone with her. Although I knew she was correct, I wasn't ready to think about anything negative. I wanted to be back on my Kyra cloud. Even if this was all a big mistake, I loved the euphoria I felt and wasn't ready to come back to reality.

Chapter 6

I sat in my car outside of The Lounge. My palms were sweating. I looked at myself in the mirror. Tara did the damn thing on my makeup. It was subtle but just enough to highlight my features. I took a shot of tequila from the flask I had in my purse. I needed to calm down. At this rate, I was liable to walk into the building and fall flat on my face.

I noticed someone walking toward my car from my peripheral. It was Morgan. She had a huge smile as she skipped toward my vehicle. Finally, she planted her hands on my window.

"Get out of the car, hooker," she yelled through the window, her breath leaving fog on it. It was colder in February than it had been during Christmas. We hit a cold spell and even got some snow. I checked my face again in the mirror, added a little more gloss to my lips, then got out of the car. "Ready to see Kyra?" She sang Kyra's name while giggling.

"Shut up. And no, I'm *not* ready. This is a mistake. I'm going home."

I opened my car door, but Morgan slammed it shut again. Then she put both of her hands on my shoulders.

"Pull it together, woman. It's not that big of a deal. It's just another night at The Lounge, a night where you might finally get fucked," she laughed.

"I really hate you." I frowned.

Morgan grabbed my arm. "Well, hate me inside. Let's go."

I followed, taking a deep breath as we reached the door.

We walked into the small performance space. The Lounge was a salsa club that allowed poets and musicians to take over on Sunday nights. The walls were splashes of bright colors, and various Hispanic flags hung from the ceiling. But on Sunday, there wasn't a Hispanic person in sight, only Black people who loved art and the random artsy white person.

Some of our friends were already sitting in our usual spot. I had an eclectic group of women I hung out with at The Lounge, primarily lesbians. I hugged everyone, trying not to notice that Kyra wasn't in the room. Our friend Cheryl walked over with a tray of small cups of wine. I was always envious of Cheryl's figure. She was also a bigger woman but carried her weight completely in her thighs and butt. She had hardly any stomach. She always dressed in fitted clothing and could rock some of the tallest pairs of heels I'd ever seen. I quickly took one of the shots. I needed something to calm me down.

We took time before the show to catch up. I had a good group of associates, but this was the main time I saw them. We all admired Temptress when she stopped to speak to us. She was once again rocking her signature 'fro with another tight bodysuit. We all made little comments about how good she looked. Many beautiful, successful, and professional women were in the building.

My feelings only intensified when I heard a familiar laugh. I stopped breathing as Kyra walked in with some of her bandmates. I felt like everything was moving in slow motion. She greeted people with head nods and her signature smile as they made their way to the stage to set up. She looked better than I remembered.

Stay calm, Paige, I thought. I didn't want to make a scene, and I wasn't ready to tell my other friends about my little secret. I was determined to play this cool. Mina's words echoed in my head. She was right. I was too excited over a mere possibility. This wasn't real yet. Kyra hadn't asked me to be her girlfriend. Hell, we hadn't spent an actual day together yet. I needed to relax. I felt like I was going to melt right out of the booth. I needed to do something to gain my composure.

"Next round is on me," I said, standing up to cheers from my friends.

I walked over to the bar. The room was starting to fill up, and the show would begin any moment. I needed at least two more shots and some in my system to maintain. I placed my order and watched the man pour the cups. The new bartender wasn't much to look at, but he was heavy with his pouring of the liquor, which I appreciated. I needed full cups of wine. I thanked him, then put a couple of dollars in the tip jar before carefully heading back to my group.

"I hope one of those is mine."

I paused. To my left was Kyra. I took a deep breath and turned toward her. She smelled like men's cologne, wearing a pair of fitted distressed jeans and a blue muscle shirt that hugged her small chest. Her arms looked incredible, and the scent made me weak in the knees.

"You are more than welcome to have one if you like," I said, hoping my voice sounded as sexy as I wanted it to.

Kyra looked me up and down. "I'm good. Hell, you are intoxicating enough."

I blushed as I looked up at her. "Thank you." I never realized just how tall she was.

"Seriously, I don't think I like your shirt. It is showing off some assets that I don't really think I want other people admiring," Kyra shifted her eyes to my chest. "Yeah, no, I don't like it. I mean, I like it, but not for other people to see."

"Shut up. I truly think no one here is looking at me," I replied.

"Girl, you really have no idea, do you?" Kyra smiled. Her eyes shifted over to the stage. "I gotta go put in this work. We'll talk later. Oh, and tell those lesbians to keep their hands to themselves." She winked at me before walking toward the bar.

I walked over to my group. I looked back to see her talking to the bartender. The bartender handed her a drink, and she walked away, greeting people as she headed back toward the stage. I took my seat and set my two new cups of wine next to me just as the host walked up to the mic. I watched Kyra as she picked up her guitar. She put the pick in her mouth. I never wanted to be a guitar pick before until now. Then the band began their rendition of "Tyrone" by Erykah Badu.

The night was amazing. The featured performer sang her ass off. During breaks, I watched my friends dance while I swayed my head to the music from the DJ. Each musical set was better than the one before it. I had to force myself not to look at Kyra. She was going in on her guitar, and I desired her even more with each song.

During the final jam, she went in for her solo. She strummed the strings so fast, her fingers moving faster than I've ever seen fingers move before.

Sweat dripped from her brow as people yelled, waved their hands, and shouted for her to do her thing. I watched her hands move swiftly with each stroke. I couldn't help but wonder what miracles she could do with those hands on my body.

I shifted my eyes to the crowd. I noticed all the eyes on Kyra as she played. Women were blushing at what I wanted to be mine. I caught myself becoming possessive. It wasn't a good look at all, so I quickly averted my eyes to my drink. I was doing too much, and I knew it.

By the end of the final song, my body no longer belonged to me. Kyra had claimed it as her own just from her subtle looks in my direction, the small smiles she flashed my way, and the winks I knew were directed at me. This woman mind-fucked the hell out of me from the stage without uttering a single word. I stayed in my seat, needing a moment to recuperate from it all. I finally forced myself to stand as my friends stood since they were about to leave.

The crowd was starting to disburse. I hovered around Morgan, who was waiting on her girlfriend to pack up her DJ equipment. I watched Kyra as she put her guitar and bass back in their respective bags while various people talked to her. By now, the crowd was almost completely gone. I knew I looked silly, still being there without reason to be. I suddenly felt awkward. What was I supposed to do at that moment? We hadn't made any actual plans. Should I leave or stay? Anxiety started to creep up on me. I knew I needed to remove myself from the situation. I hugged Morgan and started walking to the front door. At the door, I turned around. Kyra looked at me. I waved and walked out the door. I didn't want her to think I was waiting on her. Kyra needed to know I had other options . . . even if it was a total lie.

I sat outside the club in my car. The moments from the night replayed in my mind. Kyra had breaks between sets but never returned to me after our initial encounter. I had struggled to concentrate on my friends at the table with me. I was acting like a helpless fool, and I didn't like it, but I couldn't help myself.

I started my engine. I wasn't going to allow myself to become *that* girl. I needed to get home. After all, I had a synopsis due in several hours. I tried to set my focus on the task at hand, but Kyra was consuming my thoughts. I knew I was fucked. I could see her as clear as day if I closed my eyes. Those arms, her face . . . all etched in my brain. I knew I had to use it.

On the drive home, it felt like every song on the radio was catered to Kyra and me. I couldn't get her face out of my mind. I just kept reliving over and over the way she played on that stage. Finally, I made it home and immediately grabbed my computer. I called out to Alexa to play my writing mix. I feverishly typed away on my laptop until I had a finished synopsis. It was about a girl who meets a mysterious musician and gets in over her head in a sexual situation she wasn't prepared for. It wasn't my best work, but I knew it would be enough to make Mark give me the go-ahead to write the book. I sent the email and breathed a sigh of relief. But an eerie feeling rushed over me. Did I just write my own fate?

Chapter 7

Timing was a major problem for Kyra and me. We kept missing each other between my job and her musician's schedule. I was starting to worry. I wasn't hearing from her nearly as much as I did while she was on tour. It took forever for her to respond to a message, and she barely answered her phone. The worst part was that we still hadn't spent any alone time together. I'd seen her at a few events, but that always was in passing. She made sure that I was seen, throwing me winks or glances from the stage, but it was always the same after the shows. She would be with her people, almost ignoring that I existed. But by the time I always made it to my car, she would have sent me a text saying how good I looked, or she wished she could leave with me.

I was growing restless. I started to feel the "too good to be true" feeling. I knew she was busy, and being busy for an artist was a good thing. But there wasn't that much busy in the world. Even when I was busy, I could take five seconds to send a reply to a text. She was barely doing that now.

After another missed date, weeks of phone tag, and scarce texting, I decided it was time to throw in the towel. I felt horrible and found myself daily missing what we had in the beginning. I hated the idea of my friend Mina being right. Maybe she wasn't all that I thought she was. It had only been a short time, but I looked forward to speaking to her and having meaningful conversations with someone who had captured my attention. I felt robbed.

I did the only thing I could do. I threw myself into my work. I had a book release coming up that I had completely put on the back burner since meeting Kyra. I started making gift bags and new promotional ads to post online. Once I had finalized everything with the venue and catering, I moved on to working on the new book outline. Days passed, and I was starting to feel like my usual self again. But at night, when I was alone in my bed, I began to think about Kyra and what could have been.

It was a Friday night, and I was going to dedicate it to NY-style pizza and a marathon of *Sons of Anarchy*. Although I owned the complete box collection of Blu-rays, I opted to watch it on Netflix. I snuggled in for the night, ready for my favorite fictional motorcycle club, when my phone rang. I looked at the screen and gasped. It was Kyra. I caught myself from answering right away. I waited for the third ring, then answered.

"Hello," I said, sounding as uninterested as possible.

"Paige Writes," Kyra's voice filled my room from my speaker. "How are you, Miss Lady?"

"I'm good. What's up?" I pressed play on my remote.

"Good? Are you just good? I was hoping you would say you were amazing, tremendous, extraordinary, incredible. Anything but just good," she joked.

"Kyra, what's up?" I huffed.

She paused for a moment. I was sure she picked up on my attitude. "What are you doing?"

"Watching *Sons of Anarchy*."

"Without me?" She sounded genuinely shocked.

"That's a joke, right?" I could hear the irritation in my voice.

Kyra paused. She definitely wasn't ready for the attitude I was giving. We sat on the phone for a moment before she finally responded.

"Yeah, I deserve this cold shoulder treatment. I know I have been MIA, and from the inflection in your voice, I can tell you are bothered by it. Rightfully so," she replied.

"Kyra, we are grown. You can do whatever you want." I folded my arms.

"True, but that's not an excuse for my behavior. Things have just been really crazy. But I'm in Midtown, and I was calling because I wanted to see you. So, if you don't mind pausing your time in the city of Charming, can we hang out for a bit?"

My cheeks raised as a smile covered my face. She knew the city from *Sons of Anarchy,* which meant she knew the show. I took a few breaths; I didn't want to seem anxious.

"Um, I mean, what did you have in mind?" I replied as nonchalantly as I could.

"How about you come to scoop me, and we can chill out for a while? My truck is down at the moment." Kyra's raspy voice was pulling me back in.

I was taken aback by her response. I had heard that excuse before. Usually, when someone says their car "was down," it never comes back up. So it didn't sit well with me that she didn't have transportation. But I wanted to see her more than anything. Not having a car was a minor blemish I could overlook.

Kyra said she would text me where to meet her. I closed my computer and the lid to my cheesy pizza, then headed to my room to get ready. I jumped in the shower and picked out one of my favorite scents. I massaged lotion on every inch of my body in a mango body butter that matched the shower oil I used and then sprayed my body down with the matching body spray. I didn't want to overdo it with my outfit. I opted for a pair of my tighter jeans, knee-high boots, and a cute, fitted sweater I had purchased recently. Luckily, I had my hair done earlier that day, so my freshly flat ironed wrap was full of body and bounced with even the slightest move of my head. I sprayed another layer of the mango body spray over my clothes, put on my favorite red gloss, and headed out of the house.

I pulled into the parking lot of a dark, small strip mall and carefully surveyed my surroundings. It was late, and all but one of the businesses were closed. I called Kyra, who let me know she was on her way. I looked out my rearview to see where she was coming from. Why she had me meet her in such a desolate place confused me. I was a girl, by myself, in a dark and nearly abandoned strip mall. This was the setting for a horror movie.

Suddenly, I noticed a figure walking toward me. My heart began to race. That feeling quickly disappeared the moment I realized it was Kyra. Her hat, backpack, and her thick hair bounced with each step. I took several deep breaths, placed a mint in my mouth, and braced myself. She tapped on my window with her knuckles. I opened the door, and she hopped into the passenger side.

"Paige Writes." The corners of Kyra's mouth lifted, causing her deep dimple to appear on the right side. "What's up?"

"Nothing much," I said, trying to sound cool. "What's going on with you?"

Kyra gently placed her backpack on my backseat. Then she closed the door and looked over at me.

"Nothing much. Happy to finally see you." She winked her right eye at me. "Goddamn, something smells good. Please tell me it's the car and not you. 'Cause I might have to jump across this seat if this is you."

I blushed. "It's just some mango body butter."

"See?" She shook her head. "You not playing fair. How am I supposed to resist you smelling like my favorite fruit?"

"I'm sure you can control yourself," I devilishly grinned.

"I might not *want* to control myself." She winked at me again, causing my body to shiver. I shifted my body weight in my seat.

"So, was there anything in particular you wanted to do?" I asked as I started my car.

"I thought we were watching *Sons of Anarchy* or maybe *Spartacus*. But actually, no, 'cause if I watch that, I'll get hooked and end up at your house all night." Her eyes slanted, giving me a seductive glare. I noticed the smell of alcohol on her breath.

"Well, did you want to go somewhere? It's late, so we could go to like Perkins or IHOP."

"Let's just head out east. We can come up with something then," she said as she put her hand behind her head. "I'm taking over your music, though."

Kyra pulled out an auxiliary cord and put it into her phone. Then she plugged the other end into my dashboard.

"Wow, that's old school," I laughed.

"Yeah, I know. Of course, you got Bluetooth in this nice-ass car, but I don't have to do all that connecting and shit this way." Kyra scrolled through her phone. "Everybody is connected to everything these days." She smiled at me.

I felt my heart skip a beat.

We listened to music as I headed toward East Memphis. Even with my nerves taking over the best of me, I felt oddly comfortable being with her. She played different songs with guitar solos, explaining how the chords progressed. Her voice went up an octave whenever a guitar solo hit what she called "The pocket." Then I noticed the Perkins Restaurant we were approaching.

"So, did you want to get something to eat?" I asked as we reached the location.

Kyra shook her head. "Naw, let's just head to my crib. I need to do some cooking anyway," she said, bobbing her head to the beat.

I felt my whole body trembling. I wasn't expecting to go to her house, especially not on the first date. I felt panic starting to set in. I didn't want to ruin the moment we were finally having. The idea of ending our time just because I was nervous about being alone with her was absurd. I shook off the feeling and followed her directions to her apartment.

"So Paige Writes"—Kyra touched my hand, sending chills down my spine—"I am really stoked we are finally spending some QT together. I know you thought it was never gonna happen." Kyra laughed.

"No, I figured it would happen at some point. You're a busy woman, ma'am," I smiled.

"Yeah, I am so sorry about that. Trust me. I would rather spend my time with an intelligent beauty instead of around a bunch of niggas any day of the week."

I prayed my face wasn't flushed. The mix of nerves and excitement was consuming my entire body. We pulled into The Trails, an old apartment complex in the middle of what we called "Hickory Hood." I knew it well. My starter apartment was here when I was 20. I hadn't been back since, but everything looked the same, except it seemed to have more potholes than I remembered. Kyra told me where to park. As I went to open my door, she stopped me.

"Girl, you never put your hands on a door when you are with me." Kyra smiled as she hopped out of my passenger side. She grabbed her backpack from my backseat and walked over, opening my car door for me. I blushed. The couple of men I dated recently didn't ever show chivalry. I'd had women in my past do things like hold the door but never had anyone insist that I don't touch a door.

Now, I realize just how sad that really was. Kyra closed the door behind me, and I pressed my keyless entry to lock it. Then I adjusted my clothes, hoping everything was falling correctly as I followed her to her front door. Kyra opened the door and walked to the kitchen, turning on the light inside the room.

I was shocked. The place was practically empty. She had no real furniture, just two folding chairs, a drum set, and two guitars in the middle of the floor. I walked farther into the apartment until reaching the kitchen, where I just stood in the doorway.

"Did you just move in or something?" I questioned while watching her open her backpack.

Kyra shook her head. "Girl, I am a nomad. I don't need furniture and all that mess. I'm barely here."

I glanced down the hallway. The bedroom door was open. The room was empty besides a few boxes on the floor. There was no bed either.

"Wait, so you don't even have a bed? Where do you sleep?"

"I told you, nomad, baby. I had an air mattress but fucked around and got a hole. So I'm gonna buy a new one soon. But you know, sleeping on the floor isn't that bad. Great for my posture."

The entire thing seemed odd to me. I couldn't fathom living like that. Even when I lived in The Trails, I had a fully furnished apartment. The idea of her living like that worried me. I understood she was busy, but this was a bit much. However, I didn't want to press the issue. It was her house and how she chose to live. Plus, I had my own home, so it wasn't like we needed always to be here. I shrugged my shoulders and decided to change the subject.

"What do you like to cook?" I asked.

Kyra laughed. "Not *that* type of cooking," She shook her head. Then she pulled out a large bag of marijuana. "Consider me your guitarist/narcotics dealer. I gotta bag up a couple of ounces real quick if you don't mind."

"No, not at all. Go right ahead," I said, leaning against the kitchen wall. I was uneasy but tried to hide it. I was the only one among my friends who didn't smoke weed. I would partake in the occasional edible, but I just never liked the smell of marijuana. I didn't mind other people smoking, but I just didn't partake in the habit.

The smell filled the room the second she opened the large bag. Although I wasn't a smoker, I knew from the smell that it was the good stuff my friends called "loud." I watched as she measured the product before placing it into airtight bags. She was meticulous in the handling of the product.

"I've never seen a person use airtight bags for weed before," I said while watching her close the large bag.

"That's 'cause niggas are dumb. I know you smelled how loud this stuff is when I opened the bag. I am a Black woman who looks like a nigga, walking around with this nappy hair, a hoodie, and a backpack. The last thing I want is the cops coming up on me and smelling this shit. I got things to do, and they don't include jail."

"But why sell it anyway then? Aren't you taking a gamble just selling it, period?" I asked. I understood most of the world smoked it, and although legal in many places, it was still very illegal in Tennessee. I knew my friends called me square, but I just never wanted to gamble with my career, and although smoking was one thing, selling was utterly different.

"This is a temporary thing, babe. I have a goal I need to meet. But don't worry. I'll be done very soon."

"Oh, OK." I lowered my head. I felt like an idiot for even posing the question. Now I knew she was looking at me as some square chick.

"That's adorable. You're worried about me." Kyra winked at me. I couldn't help but blush.

She put the products into her backpack. Then she turned around to me. I looked up to see her staring directly at me. Our eyes met. I shifted my glance, uneasy from the interaction. Kyra took several steps closer to me. I didn't know what to do. I could feel my body trembling as she walked closer and closer until she was standing right in front of me. My comfort level was out the window by now. I had dreamed of this moment, and now my anxiety threatened to ruin it. I inhaled and attempted to exhale out the nerves. It worked for every bit of thirty seconds.

"You are a remarkable woman, Paige." Kyra ran her fingertips against my arm.

The little bit of hair on my arm stood straight up. I could feel her energy entering my flesh. I took a step to the side, moving back into the hallway. I needed to breathe and calm down.

"Well, I try," I said as I walked closer into the hallway. "I—"

I turned around to see Kyra right behind me. She walked up to me, placing both hands on my shoulders. I stepped backward as she swiftly pushed me against the wall, pinning me to it. I gasped as her lips touched my neck. My mouth fell open. I wanted to tell her to stop, but my body muted any words coming out of my mouth. Kyra nibbled on my earlobe before her lips danced down the right side of my neck before biting my collarbone. The pain only made me want more.

"You are so fucking sexy, Paige. I want you so badly," she whispered while nibbling on my earlobe again.

Yes, oh God, yes. Take me any way you want me. I tried to speak, but all I could do was gasp for air. I struggled but finally managed to get my hands on her stomach. I wanted to wrap my arms around her and pull her closer, but my hands pushed her away. I instantly regretted it, and it caught Kyra off guard.

"What's wrong? I'm sorry. Was that too forward?" she muttered as she took a few steps back.

"No, it's just—"

"No, it's too fast. I apologize." She lowered her head.

I didn't know what to feel. I had a swirling sense of euphoria sweeping through my body, but something didn't seem right. As much as I wanted her, I only knew her from our conversations. I hadn't been with a woman in so long that I didn't know if I would even be good at it anymore. Was it like riding a bike? Would it all come back to me? I didn't know much, but I knew I didn't want to fuck up the moment.

"No, don't feel bad. I loved it." I lowered my head. "I mean, I really liked it a lot. I just, honestly, I don't even know if this is something you would want in the end."

"What do you mean?" Kyra raised her head.

"Kyra, it's just . . . I'm sorry, but just you make me nervous," I said while twiddling my fingers together.

Kyra's eyes widened. "You are so adorable. We can slow down," she said as she walked back toward me. Then she put her hand on my cheek and stared deeply into my eyes. "I know it's been awhile for you, and I never want to do anything to make you feel uncomfortable."

Staring into her eyes, I felt at peace. My nerves calmed, and I loosened up. She was beautiful to me.

"You are so incredible, Paige. Such a pure spirit. You are delicate, and I need to treat you as such. I want you to feel like when I kiss you, it's because you are the only woman I want to kiss." Kyra placed her hand on my side. "When I touch you, it's because I crave you. When I eat you, it's because you are the only meal I desire."

I felt my knees trembling. Kyra didn't take her eyes off me. Instead, she slowly ran her right hand under my shirt and up my side. My body began to tremble again. I felt a huge knot forming in my stomach. I wanted her. I never wanted anything so badly in my life.

Kyra stood in front of me, her hands upon my body in the gentlest way. In her dark apartment, the only light came from the kitchen. I felt as if I were suspended in time. It was just her and me. I was there with this woman who made my soul sing. Nothing mattered; it was just us.

My eyes darted to her arms. I imagined her holding me, pulling me close to her so many times. I knew I would feel safe in those arms. I was already missing her lips. I studied their roundness. They were so soft. They felt incredible against my neck. I wondered how they would feel pressed against my lips.

"Fuck it," Kyra said as she rushed up, pushing me back against the wall. She pinned my arms against the wall above my head and pressed her lips against mine. It was happening. The one thing I couldn't stop fantasizing about was happening. My entire life, I dreamed of the moment someone would treat me like the women I loved in the old classic movies. I wanted someone to grab me, throw me against a wall, and take the kisses they desired. I was all about the moment. And this was the moment.

I submitted to her kiss. Aggressive but tender, Kyra's lips moved against mine. I lowered my lip as her tongue met mine with an unmatched fierceness. She let go of my hands, wrapping her arms around me. It felt like I had been dead or in a deep sleep my entire life. And with one kiss, I was alive. It was crazy and spontaneous, not meticulously planned like all other aspects of my life.

I put my hands in her thick hair. To my surprise, it felt as soft as cotton. I allowed my hands to get lost in Kyra's wild mane.

"Pull it," she whispered. Her breaths were growing heavier with every moment. "Grab that shit."

I gently grabbed her hair, slowly pulling it from her scalp. Kyra growled.

"Pull that shit, girl."

"I don't want to hurt you," I said.

"Baby, you can't do anything to hurt me. Do whatever feels natural. I can take it," she commanded.

Our eyes met again. I felt nerves creeping back into my body. Kyra used her index finger to lift my chin, causing our eyes to meet. She pressed her lips back against mine, pulling me close until our bodies were almost one. I decided to let go. I massaged her scalp with the palm of my hand before grabbing a handful of her hair and pulling it tight. Kyra held me closer as she aggressively kissed energy into me. I was her, and she was mine. I knew I could live in her arms.

Suddenly, Kyra pulled away from me, letting out a loud groan. She began to walk toward the front door.

"You need to go," she said aggressively as she unlocked the door.

I didn't know where that attitude came from.

"Why? Did I do something wrong?" I said, trying to stand as still as possible. I knew if I moved, my knees might buckle, and I would go down.

"Paige, you need to go because I want to fuck the shit out of you, and you are not ready for that." She opened the door.

I panicked. I didn't want to leave. I wanted more than anything to be in her arms again. But she was right. I wasn't ready to have sex with her. I had prepared myself for the possibility. My lady was waxed, and my body was covered in mango. But this wasn't how I imagined our first time. I'd fantasized about making love in a lavish hotel room, or at the least in a comfortable bed, and Kyra didn't even have an air mattress. I looked down at the brown carpet. It was the same carpet they used when I stayed there years ago. It was itchy, and I hated it. I couldn't believe they still used that same stuff. I felt queasy. I knew a vacuum was out of the question if she didn't have any furniture. Who knew the last time it was cleaned?

Hygiene aside, I knew it was too soon for my comfort. I never had sex with anyone on the first night. What would that say about me? We had been communicating for months, but this was our first time alone together. Would she think I was really that easy? What incentive would she have for continuing to get to know me if she got it on the first night? Would she want to buy the cow if she already had the milk? I knew my friends had clowned me for my beliefs. They all thought I should be as free and sexual as I wanted to be. I just never allowed myself to be that free. Was I coming off as vanilla for wanting to wait?

"Can't we just enjoy this moment?" I asked. I didn't want to leave. I had waited for what felt like an eternity to spend time with her. I wasn't ready to give it up.

Kyra shook her head. "Babe, no offense, but I'm a real-ass nigga out here. I want to fuck the shit out of you, and I can tell from your energy that you want me to fuck you too. We are adults. We can act like it now, or you can go, and we can possibly pick this up at a later date."

Possibly?

I could sense the irritation in her voice. I felt ashamed. This is what my friends told me. I never allowed myself to do what my body truly wanted. Now, this woman who had already blown my mind and had my body on a level it had never seen before was getting frustrated by my insecurities. And her words made me wonder if I left, would this be the end of us before we even began?

I thought about my friends. I could almost hear them laughing at me and my prudish thoughts. We had these conversations before. They had lectured me about how badly I needed to get laid and how I needed good sex. Was what I needed staring at me with her door open? Would walking out that door seal the fate for us? Would she look at me as a woman who knows her worth or as a scared little girl not ready for a real woman?

I felt like I was in an after-school special about peer pressure. Was she really giving me an ultimatum? Either fuck or leave and possibly never see her again? This couldn't be happening. But another piece of me thought of my friends, and she wasn't wrong. We were adults. Was I acting like a scared teenager?

We stood in the hallway with so many unanswered questions, but it wasn't the time for questions. It was time for me to decide. I closed my eyes, took a deep breath, and decided to go with my heart.

"Close the door."

Chapter 8

Kyra's eyes didn't leave me as I turned around and walked back toward the living room. I could hear her closing and locking the door and her footsteps as they slowly drew closer and closer to me. I stood still in the living room, trying to control my emotions. This wasn't nerves; this was fear. I didn't want to do this, but I felt it was now or never, and I didn't want to pass up the opportunity before me. Kyra's hands gripped both of my shoulders. I hoped she didn't feel my trembling.

As much as I wanted to be with her, I had a horrible feeling about what would transpire. But I was determined to get out of my head and out of my own way. After all, this wasn't the olden days of chaste and virgin women. I didn't know why I was making such a big deal of this. This wasn't my first rodeo. But this felt odd . . . and not in a good way. We were two adults about to do something that was supposed to be completely natural. I stood there going over all the realities, but I couldn't shake the feeling. I didn't want to do this—not like this.

There were no words. Kyra tried to pull my shirt over my head. I stopped her. Not only did I not want to do this, but I didn't want to be completely naked. I never had sex completely naked. She shook her head, pushing my hands out of the way.

"Girl, if you don't let me see what I want to see . . ."

"I don't usually get naked."

"Well, that's about to change now." With force, Kyra pulled my shirt over my head. I quickly crossed my arms over my chest. She unbuttoned my pants and pulled them down along with my panties. I stepped out of them and pushed them to the side.

"Get on the ground," Kyra commanded, and I obeyed. A few of my butterflies disappeared. I liked her forcefulness, but I was still uneasy with the situation.

Kyra disappeared to the back of the apartment. I sat on the hard brown carpet with my knees pulled into my chest. The rug was worse than I imagined. The cheap fibers poked into my backside. I tried to take my mind off it. Finally, I heard Kyra close a door. She walked back to the living room. I focused on her, watching as she removed her shirt and pants. A large black strap hung from her pelvis. My eyes widened. I didn't know what I expected, but it sure wasn't that. The object was long and thick; it had to be at least ten inches. The idea sent a shock through my body. I hadn't had a dick that size since college.

Kyra walked closer to me. Finally, she stood in front of me.

"I want to feel your mouth," she commanded.

Wait, what? I knew I was green, but not *that* green. I know she wasn't expecting me to suck a piece of plastic. Although I had to admit, I loved sucking dick, but *real* ones, *not* fake. I had heard of studs liking their women to suck their straps. I had even written about it in my lesbian book. But no woman had ever asked me to do this for real. Had I been out of the loop for that long, I didn't know the new kinks? This was weird as fuck.

"You want me to suck your . . . *that?*" I looked at the dick she had gripped in her hand.

"What did I say?" Kyra had a serious expression on her face. I was beyond confused, but I decided to do as I was told. I took her strap into my hand.

I treated it like I would any other penis. I moved my mouth, licking and flicking my tongue up and down the shaft and against the tip. It tasted like, like . . . I was sucking plastic, and I was disgusted. But Kyra let out a moan. I looked up to see her staring at me, biting her lip hard. She was really enjoying this ridiculousness. My desire to please her grew with every moan. Finally, I didn't feel horrible about what we were doing.

"Shit, babe. Shit," she moaned as her hips gyrated against the strap.

"Is this all right?" I said as I pulled away. She grabbed the back of my head.

"No, no, don't stop. I never want you to stop." She pushed my head toward the strap again. I didn't realize how much I craved dominance.

I closed my eyes and allowed myself to let things happen naturally. Before I knew it, I was into it, giving it my all just as I had done with men. I enjoyed sucking dick, but the rubbery taste wasn't appealing. But as I continued and Kyra's moans heightened, I became aroused. I looked up to see Kyra's eyes fixated on me, her bottom lip slightly hanging down as she watched what I did with a fiery intensity. I smiled inside, knowing that I pleased her.

"Shit, you about to make me cum," Kyra said as she pulled away from me. "Damn, girl."

"I'm glad you enjoyed it." I sat back, wiping the drool from the edges of my mouth. This was utterly ridiculous to me, but she was into it, so I went along with it.

I watched as Kyra pulled a condom out of her pocket. She pulled off her boxers. This I understood. Even my exes would use condoms on their straps once we were exclusive. But then it hit me. I just sucked a strap that probably had been in other women. I felt queasy at the thought but tried to get it out of my head. I was sure she washed it after each use, but I made a mental note to purchase one for her to use on only me.

I sat, bracing myself for what was coming next. I expected more foreplay before the actual act. Instead, I just went down on her strap and considering I'd been dreaming about what her mouth would feel like for months, I was ready to find out.

Kyra got on her knees and crawled to me. She gripped me around my ass, pulling me into her. I closed my eyes and held my breath as she entered me. I felt a shot of pain through my body as the tip entered. Quickly, I opened my eyes. Kyra rapidly pumped in and out. I held on to her as she fucked me hard. It was bad—terrible. She pushed her body against mine in an abrasive way. I couldn't feel anything past the initial pain from entry. This was not right at all. She grunted, pumping hard and fast. My back shifted back and forth on the brittle carpet. I tried to look at Kyra, but she wasn't looking at me. Her head was down, and her eyes were closed. It felt awful, and I wanted it to end. I kept my eyes closed and just allowed her to continue the assault on my vagina. This was worse than any man or woman I had ever been with.

Everything was wrong, and I instantly hated myself for allowing it to happen. Not only was it uncomfortable, but impersonal and cold. Where was the connection we had for the last few months? Not even the energy I felt from the kisses in the hallway was there during the actual act. I didn't feel like she was there with me at all, like I was just a pillow that she fucked on her own. As she pumped harder, I just wanted it to be over. I closed my eyes and waited for the end. Minutes later, she sped up, pumping as hard as she could before letting out a loud growl as she came.

I stared at Kyra. She immediately got up, grabbed her clothes, and walked out of the room. I lay there, confused. I pulled myself off the hard carpet and dressed as fast as possible. I put my shirt back over my head. I felt dirty and cheap. I just wanted to get home and climb into my shower. I didn't know what to do next. I figured I should wait for her to return, but I just wanted to get the hell out of Dodge. As awful as the experience was, I hoped something would happen that would at least salvage a little piece of the night. Next, I heard the toilet flush and water run. A few moments later, she returned, dressed.

"May I use your bathroom?" I muttered in a low tone.

"Yeah, of course." Kyra pointed to the bathroom. I walked down the little hallway to the bathroom, closing the door. I wanted to scream. There was nothing—no towels or paper towels, just some incredibly cheap tissue. I was disgusted by the way she lived.

I got dressed and headed back into the living room. Kyra was sitting on one of her folding chairs. She stood up and walked toward me. I smiled. She smiled back as she walked toward the front door. I couldn't believe it as she unlocked the door.

"Girl, you are. There are no words," Kyra said as I slowly made my way to the door. Then she opened it. "Look, call me and let me know you made it home."

"Um, OK." I was utterly in shock.

Kyra kissed my forehead as she let me out of the door. I walked out, expecting her to follow. But when I turned around, I heard her front door close. I thought about earlier. She didn't follow me to my car or open my car door. In an instant, I went from a woman who should never touch a car door in her presence to not even good enough to watch me walk to my car. I drove away feeling like a complete fool, and I only had myself to blame for it.

Chapter 9

I was finding things to occupy my time again. Kyra was essentially gone. It had been almost a month since our awful encounter, and things had drastically changed. Not only had we not spent time together again, but she rarely answered the phone and barely texted back. When I received a text, it was short, few, and far between. I was riddled with guilt and shame. I knew I should never have had sex with her, and now with this ghosting, I was even more upset with myself for not going with my first inclination. I finally stopped making any moves to communicate at all. Kyra needed to become a distant memory.

The hardest thing was knowing I needed to dislike her, but I couldn't make myself do it. Instead, my mind drifted back to our initial conversations and that first month of constant communication. I had to stop myself from reading our earlier DMs. I wanted that time back. I missed it desperately. How could something that felt so real be so fake in the end? My mind just couldn't make sense of it. I spent my days focusing on my upcoming release and work while trying not to allow myself to be consumed with confusion from Kyra.

I knew I needed to get over her. It was apparent she wasn't the person I thought she was. I knew there was no excuse for the way she was treating me. I felt like I was being ghosted, which was infuriating. There wasn't anything I hated more than being ghosted. It always left me wondering why, and no one should be stuck wondering what happened when a simple conversation could end things correctly. It was maddening to see her posting on Facebook about gigs and various things when she couldn't take a moment to text or call me. Finally, I had to face the harsh truth. I was just a piece of ass and gave it up way too fast.

"If that nigga was going to disappear, he was going to do it whether you fucked him the first day or in ninety days," Tara said during one of our down times at work. She had finally gotten used to using the male pronoun when talking about Kyra.

"I just feel like everything was wrong. The vibe was off. I wasn't comfortable. That's probably why I didn't enjoy it." I sighed as the whole night replayed in my mind. It did that frequently.

"But that's not your fault, Paige," Shantel turned toward me. "He is the one who didn't have any furniture. That's just like a busted fuck-nigga not to have any furniture."

I just nodded my head. I had almost forgotten Shantel wasn't aware that Kyra was a woman.

"Who doesn't have any furniture?" My coworker, Loyal, asked. He overheard our conversation while getting some coffee.

Tara took it upon herself to inform him of the situation. I was happy to get a male's opinion. Especially someone like Loyal. He was known as the office playboy. There were even rumors of his own involvement with an old lesbian coworker who had quit to move to New York after their relationship went sour.

"So let me get this right. This nigga has you in his crib, and it has no furniture at all. You gave it up, and now he doesn't call anymore," he said as he sat down in an empty chair. I couldn't help but notice how shiny his bald head was.

"Pretty much. But I will say, sh . . . He does have a hectic schedule." I caught myself quickly in hopes of a better response from him.

Loyal nodded and took another sip of his coffee.

"What do you think, Loyal, being a whore yourself? She got played, didn't she?" Tara joked with Loyal, who just shook his head.

Now, he turned his attention toward me. "Paige, do you want the *real* answer or the *nice* one?" he asked.

"Hit me with the real. I need it." I lowered my head.

"One, no man, no *real* man, is going to have an apartment with no furniture. That's *not* how we roll. We will have furniture, even if it's just to impress women. The fact that he has no car and no furniture, he's not lame—he's just full of shit. I can almost promise you he isn't laying his head there every night. That apartment is probably a front for his bullshit. I can guarantee you that is *not* where he usually resides," Loyal explained before taking another sip of coffee.

I never thought that Kyra might be living somewhere else. Maybe the apartment was just where she handled the drug or music business. It would make sense. All she had in the place were instruments. She could have a completely different apartment. That made me feel even worse. That meant that I wasn't even important enough to take to her real place.

Loyal leaned back in the chair. "OK, and second, he is not done with you. Men don't really do the 'hit it and quit it' with chicks anymore. We might make you a piece of ass, but we will hit it more than once. Especially someone like you. I mean, you *are* like a unicorn."

"Did this nigga just call you a unicorn?" Tara pointed at Loyal. We all laughed.

"Listen, Paige is a talented, intelligent, articulate, beautiful woman with no kids. She has her own home and career, actually, multiple careers.

On top of that, she is also damn near untouched."
Loyal continued. "You are the type a dude either
wants to marry or take advantage of."

"But why take advantage of her?" Shantel asked.

"Right. Why take advantage of a good woman?
Then complain when we turn savage?" I frowned.
It was the story of my life. I just hadn't figured out
the savage part yet.

"Because he probably knows you are going to
catch feelings quickly. He thinks his dick is the answer to all, and you said he's a musician, so women
are throwing it at him all the time. You don't have
much to compare it to." Loyal stood up.

"So, you're saying what I thought: He just used
me for some ass?" I crossed my arms, upset by the
whole situation.

"I'm saying that you have to play the game. Trust
me. He *will* be back. Probably the moment he feels
you are sick of his shit. If he contacts you, answer
but don't agree to meet with him. You have to show
him that you have other options outside of him.
And you are going to hold him accountable for his
actions."

Loyal walked over to me, put his hands on my
shoulders, and looked me directly in my eyes. I
could see why women in the office fell for him. He
was very charismatic. It made me further question myself. If Loyal could stare at me with his best
bedroom eyes and I did not feel anything, maybe I
was more than just *a little* curious.

"The last thing to remember, work on your poker face. Right now, you look like a chick in love."

"I am *not* in love." I threw my hands up in protest. Loyal calmly put his hands on top of mine and lowered them.

"I didn't say you were in love. I said you *look* like you're in love. Do not fall in love with this man. But if you are already in love with him or feel like you are close to being in love—stay away from him. From everything you have said, he is *not* the one. You gotta get your feelings in check. If anything, he should be nothing more than a random hookup. Do *not* expect anything more from him," he said with a stern expression on his face.

I nodded. Loyal joked with Tara for a minute before heading back to his desk. His words replayed in my mind. He was right. Whenever Kyra texted me, I answered immediately. And when she contacted me after a long absence, I responded fast. The truth was, I lived for those moments, and the excitement of finally having a moment with her made me want them even more.

Life had taken a drastic turn. I dreaded the end of my workday. At least at work, my coworkers kept me entertained. I couldn't focus on writing anything I wanted to put out. I was a mess, and I knew it. I had to do something before I completely lost my mind.

I made it home and retreated to my usual spot in my chair in the living room. Then my cousin Devon called me. Of course, I welcomed any call at that point.

"Hey, cuz," I answered, trying to sound as upbeat as possible. "What's crackalackin?"

"Hey, do you have any plans this weekend? And can you get off on Friday?" she replied.

I sat up in my chair. "Yeah, I can get off. What's up?"

"Want to go with me to New Orleans to meet April and Kristen? I know it's short notice, but it's Kristen's birthday, so we're all going down. The guys will be there too."

I jumped up. "Um, hell yeah. What time are we leaving? Do you need me to drive or what?"

Devon laughed. "Someone is excited. We'll leave at 8:00 a.m. I'm getting a rental. Are you sure you can get off? I know it's only two days from now."

"Dev, you could have called me Friday morning, and I still would have said yes." I did a fist pump.

I hung up the phone and ran to my room. This was *just* what I needed. My cousins were amazing, and our weekends were always fun. I hadn't been to New Orleans in years. I knew I needed to do something, and traveling was always my escape from tragic reality.

I posted that I was going to New Orleans on my Facebook page. Then I started picking out what outfits I would take with me. Finally, I had something to take my mind off the enigmatic musician. If my cousins couldn't get my mind off her with their antics and the liquor of Bourbon Street, nothing would work.

Suddenly, I heard my instant messenger notification chime. I turned my phone on to see Kyra's name. Quickly, I dropped my phone on the bed. I didn't need to read her message. I knew if I read it, I would reply immediately. I also knew that just opening it would let her know I read it. I hated that feature about messenger.

I continued to pack and listen to music. My messenger notification chimed again. I walked over and picked up my phone. Now, I had three messages from Kyra. I couldn't resist. I had to read them.

Kyra: Hey. I'm in Midtown. Are you busy?

I just stared at the message.

Kyra: Guess so.

I stared at the messages and rolled my eyes. I wasn't falling for it again. She was not about to get a free ride and some free ass from me just because she let me know she was in my neighborhood. I felt an overwhelming sense of pride in myself. I could handle her.

Paige: Sorry, was packing. What's up?

I immediately saw the writing dots moving.

Kyra: Yeah, I miss your face. Can I come over? I can help you pack.

This was the test. I could say no and tell her to fuck off. But a bigger part of me wanted to see her. I wanted to be petty, have her walk into my beautiful house, and feel awful for having me lie on that old carpet that gave me carpet burn. I also knew I could have her here and totally deny her any access to any parts of my body. Although our sexual experience was horrible, I couldn't forget about her lips and how passionate the kisses were. Then I thought about what Loyal said to me. This wasn't the plan. I wasn't supposed to agree to see her. But I couldn't make myself say no. I didn't want to have sex with her, but I yearned to kiss her again and be in her arms. Plus, I did miss our conversations more than anything. I could do this. I could have her over and not have sex. That would be easy.

I sent Kyra my address.

Chapter 10

I hopped in the shower to freshen up. I opted for my favorite mango scent since she loved it so much the last time. Then I turned on my wax burner and allowed the ocean breeze fragrance to fill my home. I analyzed my closet looking for the perfect outfit. I wanted something sexy, but sexy wasn't my forte. I was more of a jeans and cute tops girl. I dug to the back of my walk-in closet and found a wrap maxi dress I'd bought but never wore. It was the perfect mix of sexy and semi casual. I could play it off as a loungewear dress. I set my playlist to my favorite soul playlist and waited to see if she would show up. A few minutes later, I heard a knock at my door.

I took a quick look at myself in my mirror and doused myself in the matching mango body splash to go with the body butter I put on earlier. Then before I headed to the door, I opened my computer, turned to an open document I was working on, and set it on my couch. I didn't want Kyra to know I was waiting for her or that I took the time to prepare for her. Nope. I wanted to come off as working while looking casually hot. Then I walked to the door, took one last deep breath, and opened it. Kyra stood there with her hair braided in corn-rows and a baseball cap on her head. I held the door open as she walked into the house.

"Hey, beautiful," she said as she hugged me. Kyra took a giant whiff of my neck. "Smelling good again. I'ma start calling you Miss Mango."

"Cute," I smirked as I closed the door behind her.

"Man," Kyra looked at me with a grin as she walked into my house. She focused on the large canvas prints of my book covers lining my corridor wall. "These books are the shit," she replied.

"Thanks."

She stopped in front of my one lesbian book. Kyra pointed at the book and grinned. "I still need a follow-up to this one."

"Working on it," I said in the driest voice I could muster. "This way to the living room."

We walked down my corridor until we reached my comfortable living room. I motioned for her to sit on my large sectional.

"Would you like something to drink?" I asked as she made herself comfortable on the edge of the sectional.

"Mmm, watcha got?" She smiled. I wasn't going to let her adorable, devilish grin get to me this time.

"Um, some of everything. Wine, whisky, vodka, rum. No gin."

"Cognac?"

"I actually have some Pure White Hennessy I brought back from Mexico."

Kyra's eyes widened. "Oh, word? I've heard so much about that but never tried it. Yes, I'd love some of that."

I walked into the kitchen and grabbed a bottle of Merlot and Hennessy. I realized I didn't think it out well as I had no way to hold both a wineglass and cognac glass.

"Need a little help in here?" Kyra startled me as I turned around to see her standing in the doorway.

"Actually, yeah, I could." I used the wine opener and popped the cork. She grabbed both bottles, and I took the glasses. Then we walked back to the living room.

Kyra looked around my living room. "Paige Writes, your house is phenomenal. But I wouldn't expect anything less from my favorite author."

I caught myself blushing. "Thanks, it's my fortress of solitude."

"Naw, you can't be up in here by yourself. This is a showpiece. It should be shown off."

"I have people over sometimes. My friends come over. I love my house. It's my special place, where I can be completely free. I can go out to be around people."

"You know what? I feel that." Kyra took a swig from my wine bottle. "This is good."

"Thanks, I got it in Rome," I replied. "I tried some in Venice and just had to bring back a few bottles. I had the store ship me a case. I'm down to my last three bottles." I realized I was rambling as we sat down.

"Oh, no wonder I can't understand shit on the label." She laughed.

I smiled, not giving her the satisfaction of an actual laugh. Then I picked up my computer and pretended to be interested in whatever was on my screen. I snuck a glance at her as she opened the bottle of Hennessy and poured herself a little. Kyra took a sip, savored it, and nodded.

"Yeah, yeah, this is some *good* shit."

"Glad you like it. I only got it for when my guy friends are over. They are the only ones who seem to love to drink it."

"Well, add me to that list." She poured more to fill her glass. I was shocked. I'd never seen anyone pour a full glass without adding something to mix with it. No wonder she smelled like liquor the last time we were together. She was a heavy drinker.

"So, wait, did you say you were packing?"

"Yeah, I'm headed to New Orleans in two days."

Kyra smiled. "Aw, shit, that's my spot. I had a lot of gigs there once, and I love it. I might make that my next move one day. I could totally see myself living there."

"Yeah, I could see that. The music scene is like no other."

Kyra took another big sip from her glass. "You got that right. So yeah, I could definitely see myself living there one day."

I sipped my wine. "It was a last-minute trip for me. Just getting away with my peeps for two nights."

"I feel ya. See, you should have invited me. Then we could have really turned up. Hit some great music spots, and I could see how you move."

Kyra winked at me. It was a struggle, but I held my composure.

"I mean, you're so busy, I doubt you would have had time for this. After all, we've barely spoken recently." I shrugged my shoulders as I took another sip of my wine.

Kyra's eyes locked on me. I could feel the tension mounting in the room. She put her glass on a coaster on my coffee table. "So, Paige. I need to apologize again to you," she muttered.

I glanced up from my screen to see her staring at me.

"I know I have been MIA again." She lowered her head.

"Look," I said, putting down my computer, "there's no need to do this. I'm a big girl. I understand what this is or was."

Kyra looked confused.

"Obviously, we had different intentions in mind. I thought you were serious when you told me you were looking for something real—"

"I am," Kyra cut me off. "Paige, please don't think I was feeding you game. It's not like that. It's like . . ." She stood up. "It's like this amazing woman comes into my life, we have this fantastic experience, and then my life goes to complete shit."

"What do you mean?" I asked while taking a sip of my wine, bracing myself to hear this explanation.

Kyra paced my floor holding her cognac glass. "Babe, you have no idea what has happened in my life. First, I went to jail."

"What?" I sat up. "Weed?"

"Naw, some civil court stuff. Plus, I got this little job to help me out a bit, and I think they will get rid of me already. The manager is a bitch. I mean, I've literally been hit with a mountain of shit, and I didn't want to include you in any of that. But I felt bad because we had that incredible night, and then I couldn't be around."

"You thought the night was incredible?" I frowned by mistake. I never imagined what I thought was terrible, she could think was actually good.

"Hell yeah,"—Kyra sat down next to me—"Girl, you have been wasting your God-given talent. The sex was amazing, but your head . . . That shit was off the charts phenomenal."

I turned to Kyra. "Okay, you gotta explain this to me. What exactly do you get out of me sucking a piece of plastic?"

Kyra giggled. "It's a mental thing but also physical. The motions you make against my pelvis cause a fantastic sensation. But honestly, it's more mental than anything. Watching you submit to me . . . sexy as fuck."

I couldn't hold back my blushing this time. The few men I had been with always said I gave amazing head but never to that point. I felt bad. The look on her face let me know she was serious. I wish I felt the same way.

Kyra instantly picked up on my hesitation. "Wait, did you not enjoy yourself?"

My first reaction was to lie, but I couldn't let the words come out of my mouth. I felt that if I lied to her, she would instantly see right through it.

"Honestly, it was just a little uncomfortable being on that carpet. And I just think I was in my head too much." I shrugged my shoulders. "I mean, I never enjoy sex, so it's not a big deal."

Kyra picked up her drink and joined me on the chaise half of my sectional. "What do you mean you never enjoy sex?"

"I don't know how to explain it. I've had good experiences, but the way people obsess about it, that's just never been me. I never had an experience making me go crazy for it. It's overrated to me." I took another sip of wine.

"Babe, I feel horrible. I fucked up. I was drunk and a little high that night and wanted you so bad that I didn't consider you the way I should have. Here I am, thinking you loved it as much as I did. I gotta do better. I'm going to make it my responsibility to make you enjoy it. I *will* make that up to you." Kyra picked up my hand and kissed it.

I felt the swell of emotions I had for her resurfacing as if they had never left. I needed something to break the heat growing between us. I liked her, but I wasn't going to give in the way I did the time before. So I grabbed my remote and turned on the television to see *Boomerang* was on.

Kyra was just as passionate about films as I was. First, she explained parts of the movie I never noticed. Then she pointed out how the light on the Empire State Building goes on and off when Eddie Murphy has key moments. I found myself smiling, hanging on her every word. I loved seeing the excitement on her face. She was comfortable and having a good time just chilling and watching the movie with me.

We watched the movie while talking and laughing throughout it. As Eddie Murphy confessed his love to Halle Berry at the end, I wondered what the rest of the night would bring. A piece of me wanted Kyra to try something so that I could say no. But deep down, I knew no was not going to be my answer.

As the credits began to roll, Kyra stretched her arms before standing up. I anticipated what might happen next. Being in my fortress of solitude, I was ready for anything.

"Well, this was dope, Paige Writes. We gotta pick this up soon."

"Oh, you heading out?" I responded, trying not to sound disappointed.

"Yeah, I got a long day tomorrow. But don't fret. I'll be back soon." She gave me her signature wink.

I was disappointed but wasn't going to let her know. Of course, I wanted her to stay, but the fact that she didn't try anything gave me hope. Maybe Loyal was wrong. Maybe Kyra had a lot going on and wanted to be with me. After all, she might look like a dude, but she was still a woman. So, could I take a man's advice when it came to her?

"So, you heading to New Orleans without me?" Kyra said.

"Yeah, but like I told you, it's just a quick trip with my cousins," I said as she took my hand, helping me stand.

"Have fun, but do me a favor and check out something other than Bourbon. New Orleans has a lot to offer, and most of it isn't on Bourbon. At least go to Frenchman."

Kyra grabbed her backpack. She held my hand as we walked to the front door. Then she wrapped her arms around me and held me tight. I felt safe in her arms. I didn't want to leave them. She planted a kiss on my forehead before leaving. I closed the door and touched my forehead. There was no denying it. With one night, she had me all over again. I knew Kyra was the one I wanted. I just hoped she truly felt the same way.

I headed back into my living room to straighten up before I called it a night. Then I grabbed my wine bottle and glass and looked over to get the bottle of Pure White. I looked around the table, but it wasn't there. So I paused for a moment. Then finally, I picked up the phone and called her.

"Missing me already?" Kyra answered. I could hear the wind from her windows rolling down in the background.

"You wish," I giggled. "Hey, where did you put the bottle of Pure White? I don't see it."

"Oh, I thought you heard me when I said I was taking it. Did you not hear me?"

I paused. "Um, no, I don't remember hearing you say that at all."

"It's not a problem, is it?"

I wanted to tell her yes. I tried to think if I had heard her and didn't remember. "No, it's cool. I just thought I was crazy over here for a moment."

Kyra laughed. "Yeah, girl, I really like it. I mean, I finished half the bottle anyway."

"Right. About that, let me know if you made it home safely, please."

"Will do."

I hung up the phone. As I washed the glasses, I couldn't help but replay the night in my head. I didn't remember her asking for the bottle. I didn't know if she did, and I didn't remember, or if she just took it. Finally, I shook it off. It wasn't that serious for me to concern myself over. I had another two bottles anyway. I wasn't going to let some liquor mess up my great night. I was on cloud nine, and nothing was going to change that for me.

Chapter 11

New Orleans was just the break I needed. The atmosphere of music and food spoke to my spirit in a way I didn't know I needed. I also didn't realize how much I missed spending time with my cousins. We had one full day to enjoy the city and planned on enjoying every moment.

While my cousins spent the morning sleeping in after spending the first night on Bourbon Street, I decided to take in the city's sights. I loved getting lost walking down the streets, seeing the houses, and passing through the cemeteries with their large aboveground tombs and wall vaults. I read a few names, crafting stories in my head about how they lived and died. Soon, I stopped at a little coffee shop on a corner and grabbed a latte and scone. It felt good to be alone with my thoughts, even if most of those thoughts were about Kyra.

Kyra was communicating with me the entire time. We texted throughout the day, mostly her asking about everything I was doing while also recommending things for me to do and eat. I loved the communication, but I also took Loyal's advice. I took breaks from responding to her, making sure she wasn't the only thing on my mind, even if it wasn't entirely true. It seemed to be working. She contacted me the way she did in the beginning, making jokes, flirting, and making me feel desired. I was eating it up but making sure not to fall too hard into it.

Day turned into night, and my cousins and I headed out to party. I took Kyra's advice, and we headed to Frenchmen Street to hit some night-clubs. First, we went into Maison, where a live band played jazz renditions of soul classics. I watched with a drink in my hand as my cousins hit the dance floor with some local men who had flirted with them while we waited in line. I wasn't a dancer, so I enjoyed the bottles that the men purchased for them.

An hour and five drinks later, I was faded. My body swayed from right to left in our booth. Then the band started a rendition of "Before I Let Go" with a Zydeco flare. I bounced in my seat as I poured another drink.

"Looks like you need someone to dance with, baby."

I turned to see a slightly pudgy male with a shiny gold tooth in my face. I was feeling so good I smiled at him.

"Thank you, but I'm not a dancer."

"Could have fooled me." The man pulled out one of our chairs and helped himself to a seat. "Can I know your name?"

I felt my phone vibrate in my pocket. "My name is Paige," I said as I pulled out my phone from my pocket.

"Beautiful name. Can I buy you a drink?"

I looked down at my phone and saw a message from Kyra on my screen.

Kyra: Hope you're having fun in N'awlins. I'm missing you like crazy.

I smiled at the text message. My heart was bursting with joy. I didn't know what had changed, but I loved being back on track with her.

Paige: Missing you too.

"So how 'bout that drink, sweetheart?" the man asked with a smile.

I sighed. "Thank you, but I shouldn't. I'm with someone."

I knew we weren't official, but it was only a matter of time. And I loved how it sounded to say that I belonged to Kyra.

Chapter 12

"Bish, you about to kill it tonight," Tara said as she patted eye shadow on my face. It was the night of my book release party, and I wanted everything to be perfect. And since I knew I would take many pictures, I let Tara take care of my makeup and hair.

"Please, don't overdo it. It's a book party, not a club event."

"Girl, it's your night. You are *supposed* to look extra fabulous."

I couldn't disagree with her on that. I had been working on this event for months, and it was finally here. The tickets sold out quicker than I imagined. I planned everything from the menu to the decor. I picked the perfect venue, a little boutique hotel rooftop bar and lounge. I wasn't big on many things, but I always went out for my book releases and my birthday. Even some local press would cover the event this time, which was new. Although my books were very well known in the African American urban fiction world, they hadn't hit major success the way many felt they should. But I wasn't going to think about numbers or bestsellers' lists. I just wanted to have a great night and celebrate my accomplishment.

"All right, you're ready," Tara said as she turned me around toward her mirror. I opened my eyes to see my face beat for the gods.

"Oh, wow. Wow. Damn, I look good," I squealed.

"I told you. Now, throw that dress on, and I'm going to get dressed, and then we can head out."

I quickly dressed. I found a black skater dress that I loved, but Tara insisted I go with some color. So I picked a red skater dress with lace and rhinestone embellishments on the top. I had to admit, I looked good, even if I was out of my comfort zone.

We headed up the elevator to the rooftop. My mouth dropped when I saw the large crowd. They all turned and started clapping as I walked out. I lowered my head. Even with the party for me, I found it hard to accept the admiration.

I was ushered over to my custom step and repeat. I loved seeing my name and the book on the giant backdrop. People lined up to greet me and take photos. Although I had been practicing my smile for weeks, I didn't want a single picture to come out with me looking goofy. I thanked each person and stood there, nodding and smiling as they gave me their well wishes and thoughts. I humbly thanked them and smiled for more photos.

The lights and my taller-than-normal wedges were quickly taking their toll. Soon, I felt myself getting light-headed.

I turned to walk away when I felt a tap on my shoulder. I turned around and gasped. Kyra stood in black jeans and a blue button-down with her hair pulled in a high bun. I mentioned the event to her but never expected her to show up. Our conversations were back on track, but I hadn't seen her since I returned from New Orleans almost a month ago. But I wasn't too disappointed as I had a lot on my plate between work, writing, and putting the finishing touches on this event.

"Can I get a picture with the famous Paige?" Her deep dimples appeared as she held her arms out. I embraced her.

"Wow, I didn't expect to see you tonight."

"Why not? I told you I was coming. I had to be one of the first to get my hands on this book." We turned to the photographer who snapped our photos.

"Paige!" I looked over to see an old coworker named Missy walking up to me with her date. She looked at Kyra. "Kyra, hey, how are you?" She hugged Kyra. I couldn't help but notice the surprised expression on Kyra's face. "Small world. I didn't know you all knew each other."

"Of course, I know Paige. I'm a huge fan of her work." Kyra gave Missy a quick hug.

"Thanks for coming, Missy. Wait, let's all get a photo." I smiled as I turned back to the photographer. We all stood for the photo.

"Well, I am excited about this book, honey. You know I love your work." Missy turned to her tall date, a handsome man, her blond curls bouncing with every movement of her head. "I worked with Paige. She would be writing while at work. I read one of her books and couldn't put it down."

I felt myself getting light-headed again.

"Well, you guys please enjoy the party. Try the signature drink," I said to Missy and her date. They walked away, and I noticed a few more people heading toward me. I needed a break but didn't want to disappoint anyone.

"Paige . . ." Kyra put her hand on the small of my back. "Babe, you look flushed. Have you eaten anything today?"

"No, I haven't." I noticed the concerned expression covering her face.

"Yeah, okay." Kyra guided me away from the step and repeat and toward the table set up for me to sign books. A few people tried to stop me, but she intervened, ensuring they knew she was running things at that moment. Kyra pulled my chair out. "Sit down. I'll get you something to drink and eat."

I watched as she disappeared into the crowd. Then Morgan walked over and sat next to me.

"Wow, would you look at y'all?" Morgan grinned.

"I know. I really didn't expect her to make it. Figured she would have a gig."

"Well, I'm glad she did. And the way she's catering to you, I hope she keeps it up." Morgan patted my shoulder before standing up. "I'm going to get another drink."

A few minutes later, Kyra appeared with a plate of food and a bottle of water. She set the food in front of me, then opened the water and handed it to me.

"Drink some of this first. You gotta do better, boo. Can't have you being dehydrated at your own party."

"Thank you, Kyra. I didn't realize that I hadn't eaten."

"No problem, baby. I'm here for you. Now, eat before the crowd appears again."

I motioned to the seat next to me. "Hey, wanna sit down?"

Kyra shook her head. "Naw, this is your night. You need to be on display. Eat something and get back to your party. I'll be around." She winked at me. I blushed as she walked off.

The rest of the event went seemingly well. I mixed and mingled with fans and friends. I did a quick interview with the Arts columnist for the local newspaper before sitting down to sign books for practically all the people at the event. I scanned the room frequently, trying to spot Kyra. She was making her rounds, talking to different people she knew. It felt special having her there. She kept her distance but checked on me from time to time, bringing me water and one of my signature drinks.

I had thought of us being together all the time, but I never considered the long-term options. Kyra knew exactly how to act as a partner at an event. She didn't hover or try to make the event about her. Even when standing near me, she gushed about me to various people who came up. She was a breath of fresh air. Being an artist, she knew how to act in these situations. I thought about when I was dating a girl at one of my other events. She got upset when I didn't give her the time she felt she deserved. Kyra didn't have that issue. She was able to mingle with people and allow me to have my moment. I respected her even more for that.

Two hours in and the DJ called for me to come to the front. He handed me a mic to say a few words to the crowd. My hands immediately started to sweat. I could write all day long, but speaking in front of a group always made me nervous. He made the announcement, and suddenly, all eyes were focused directly on me. I tapped the mic to make sure it was on.

"I just wanted to take a moment to thank everyone for coming out tonight. I might be a woman of many words on paper, but not aloud. But you all taking the time to come out really means the world to me, and I hope each of you enjoys this new book. Now, enough of me. Get drunk and have fun."

The crowd gave me a round of applause that made me blush. I thanked people offering me more well wishes as I walked over to my group of friends. I quickly scanned the crowd but didn't see Kyra. I hoped she hadn't left without saying anything to me. Then as I started to worry, I spotted her talking to the local poet from the scene. I let out a sigh of relief. I knew it was crazy that I was so worried about her at my own event, but I just was happy that she was here.

The night was in full swing, people were dancing, and everybody had a great time. I was talking with a group of women when I felt Kyra's hand on my back. I turned my head and smiled at her.

"Excuse me, ladies, but do you mind if I pull this talented creature away for just one moment?"

We took a couple of steps away so we could be alone. Then Kyra pulled me into her arms. She held me tight as she spoke in my ear.

"I gotta run, but this night was everything."

My smile faded. "Oh, so soon? Things are just getting really hype."

"Yeah, got some stuff to take care of. But this was great, you are great, and you look fucking fantastic." Kyra kissed me on my cheek. "I'll hit you later. Enjoy your night, and make sure you hydrate."

I watched as she walked away until I couldn't see her anymore. I was bummed but didn't have the time to think about it. Within seconds, someone else was trying to get my attention. I put on my happy face and headed back to my party.

Chapter 13

After my book release party, things seemed to take a turn for the better. Kyra called and texted more frequently, mostly at night during her events. I wished it was all day but realized that was just me being greedy for her time. She made sure I knew her gig schedule. She was a part of the house band at a local restaurant on Mondays and Wednesdays, while weekends changed from week to week. The other nights were used for practicing with the two bands she was a member of. I looked forward to the notification I set up for her text messages. Like clockwork, they came right around seven or eight o'clock.

I took a break from my new book outline to scroll on Facebook and Instagram. Suddenly, I stopped on a flyer for an event at Soul Slice, a local Black-owned pizza lounge. I was shocked to see Kyra's face at the bottom with the message "K Strums Birthday Celebration." I quickly sent her a message.

Paige: Your birthday is in three weeks? Why didn't you tell me? I didn't realize our birthdays were so close together.

I waited for a response, but nothing came.

Paige: You were almost cool enough to be a Cancer, but damn, you just had to be a Gemini.

I continued to wait but still no response. I figured she must be busy, so I decided to get right to the point.

Paige: Do you want me to come?

The chat babbles appeared to let me know she was typing. They stopped for a moment, then started back. I waited in anticipation for her response.

Kyra: Yeah, but it's not a big deal. No, I don't want you to come. I'd rather just see you later.

Her response instantly put me off. Why would she not want me to come to her birthday party?

Kyra: I legit don't want to go myself. But I wouldn't mind celebrating a little with you.

I smiled.

Paige: Sounds good to me.

I loved birthdays and always did them in a big way. I had worked hard to make Kyra's birthday special a few months before. After weeks of vetting her to get info on the things she liked, I finally came up with an idea. Unfortunately, the woman was a closed book. She continued to tell me that she didn't care and wasn't good at accepting gifts. I told her not celebrating was not an option, especially after she showed up for my book party. I wanted to do something to show her how much I cared and appreciated the effort she made.

Things were still not ideal. There would be days and sometimes weeks that we barely spoke, and our alone time was still mostly nonexistent. Outside of my party, I only saw her at The Lounge, where we kept things very civil. She would speak but spend most of her time on stage or around her bandmates. Most of our conversations were through text, which was still scarce sometimes. So I was surprised when she popped up at my home twice within that month for a few hours. We spent that time talking and watching random things on TV. I wasn't a fan of her popping up on me. If it weren't for my video doorbell, I wouldn't have any time to at least spray a little body splash on me before she walked in. But at this point, I was happy to have the little bits of time with her. We had yet to get back involved sexually, which was all right with me. But I did miss hugging her, and I definitely missed kissing her. Outside of a forehead or kiss on the cheek, I hadn't had her lips on mine since that night at her house.

Kyra had to work on her birthday, so she made plans to come over a few days later. When she walked into my house, I made her stand in the hallway while I prepared her surprise.

"Come in," I yelled as I lit the final light.

Kyra's face lit up at the sight of the sparklers on mini-bundt cakes. She laughed, clapping her hands as she walked over to the spread. On the table were five miniature cakes, each with a different flavor.

"Babe, are you serious right now?" she asked as she picked up a chocolate cake.

"Well, I tried to get you to tell me your favorite cake flavor, but since you wouldn't, I just decided to get you one of each." I smiled.

"Oh my God, this is amazing." She pinched a piece off, put it in her mouth, and then closed her eyes to enjoy the dessert.

"If there are any that you don't want, just let me know. Of course, I didn't expect you to like them all."

Kyra put up her hand. "Baby, I told you I am a fat girl at heart. There is no such thing as a type of cake that I don't like." Her accent came out strong in her reply.

We sat on the couch, and I watched as she devoured the mini-cake, savoring each bite. I was delighted to see her so happy. I couldn't wait for her to get the rest.

"OK, so now, it's present time." I picked a gift bag up from the side of my couch.

Kyra's eyes widened. "There's more? Are you kidding me?" she said with a mouth full of cake.

I handed her a bag. She pulled the tissue paper out, pulling out a black book bag. I grinned from ear to ear as she admired the bag.

"I know you love your backpack, but I noticed it was old, so I got you this bag. It's for musicians. It has special compartments for your stuff," I explained while pointing out the various zippers.

"This is . . . Baby, this is perfect. I can take this on the road with me." Kyra continued to admire the bag.

"You gotta open each part," I told her, trying to hold in my excitement.

Kyra began opening the various compartments. She pulled out different mini-bottles of liquor and laughed.

"Again, you wouldn't tell me your favorite liquor, so I just got a variety," I said while watching her open the gift. She opened another compartment to find a gift card to the Memphis Music Shop.

"Are you serious? I will *so* be using this." Kyra pulled her worn-out wallet out and put the gift card in it. Had I known it looked that bad, I would have also gotten her a wallet.

"There is one more thing." I motioned for her to open the main compartment. I was most excited for her to open this gift.

She pulled out a small book I had bound together. As she read the title, her mouth dropped open.

"I wanted to show how much I believe in you. So I took your poetry and writing from your Facebook notes, formatted them, and had them bound into this book. See, Kyra, you said you didn't think you could write a book. So I wanted to show you that you could . . . and have."

Kyra held the book in her hands. I couldn't read her facial expression. Her lips were pressed tightly together. She just stared at the book. Finally, she opened it, admiring each of her musings in print. Then she turned her head toward me.

"Paige, you have no idea how much this means to me. Seriously, no one has ever done anything this thoughtful. I mean, I love the cakes and even the liquor. But *this,* I will treasure this for the rest of my life."

Kyra put her hand on my cheek. I gently rubbed my face against her palm. It was softer than I remembered. Then her hand moved to the back of my head. She slowly pulled me closer until we were entirely in each other's space. I breathed in her smell, clean but with a hint of something woodsy. I shivered. Kyra looked me in my eyes, studying me as if she were searching for something there. I wanted her to find the truth in my eyes. The truth was, I was falling in love with her, even though we didn't get much quality time.

Kyra nudged my chin up with her thumb. I was drawn to her lips. She bent in as I closed my eyes. Our lips met as she caressed my mouth with her own. This was different from all the other kisses. This wasn't about sex. It was so much more. Kyra cupped the back of my back, kissing me more deeply than ever before. I could hear her heart beating. We were in sync.

The kiss lengthened, deepened, and became more passionate as we melted together. I held her arms, hoping she didn't feel my body trembling. Suddenly, Kyra gripped my arms and pushed me back.

"Maybe we need to stop," she whispered. She dropped her head and exhaled. "I told you the next time I wanted things to be perfect for you."

Nothing mattered. I wanted to show her what those words meant to me more than anything. She cared. That was all I needed to know. I pressed my index finger against her lips.

"This is your birthday. It's all about you."

We were silent. Finally, Kyra stood up. I looked at her as she held her hand out.

"Well, in that case, come with me."

Kyra took my hand. I followed her as she led me to my bedroom as if I didn't know where it was. My heart was racing, but this felt different. I wanted it this time, which made the moment that much more exciting.

As soon as we entered the room, it dawned on me. We weren't at her house, so she wouldn't have her strap. I got worried. How would I please her now? I didn't know if she was a touch-me-not woman who didn't want to be pleased by her mate or if she would allow me to go down on her. I was so used to studs who didn't let me touch them that the thought of giving her head or anything never actually crossed my mind. I wanted her, but I didn't know if I was ready for that.

Kyra placed her hand on the back of my head. She leaned in and kissed me. "Lie back," she commanded, and I obeyed.

Kyra walked out of the bedroom. I wondered what she was up to. I saw my bathroom light come on. She emerged a few moments later, wearing her strap and sports bra. I couldn't help but smirk. She came prepared. Kyra walked over to the edge of the bed. This time, I was ready. I inched closer and took the strap in my hand. Up and down, I bobbed my head. Kyra pushed my head down as deep as it could go. I breathed through my nose until I couldn't take anymore. Finally, I pulled back, struggling to catch my breath. Tears fell from my eyes. Kyra wiped them with her hand.

"You are amazing, Paige," she reassured me, only making me want her more.

I took her strap back into my mouth and stroked it rapidly as my mouth moved up and down the shaft. Kyra let out a raspy growl that caused her legs to tremble. That was new. Kyra pulled away and paced the floor for a moment before turning back to me. I waited in anticipation for what was coming next.

Then Kyra gently pushed me back on the bed. I positioned my head on my pillows as she pulled my underwear from under my maxi dress. Kyra climbed on the bed, her head disappearing under my dress. A moment later, she pulled her head back out.

"If you don't take off this shit . . ." she huffed. "I want to see you, all of you."

I nervously pulled the dress over my head. Kyra unhooked my bra with ease, allowing my F breasts to fall. I tried to cover them, but that was impossible. She pushed my arms on the bed by my head and then forcibly kissed me. I loved it. My body responded by grinding against her. Lowering one hand, she placed her index finger inside of me.

"Damn, baby, you so wet," she purred as her finger moved swiftly inside me. I closed my eyes. It felt so good I didn't want it to end.

Before I knew it, I felt a slight pain as she entered me with her man. Kyra kissed me as her hips ground against me. I let out a moan of pure ecstasy. This was different from the last time. This felt incredible.

Kyra went deeper and deeper as her mouth explored my lips and my breasts. She licked all around my nipples, stopping only to suck on them in motion with the work she was putting in with her manhood. I felt a deep sensation creeping through my body until a tidal wave of heat exploded from me. Kyra moved faster and faster as I came until she let out a loud release.

Finally, she rolled over to the side of my bed.

"Goddamn, girl. What you trying to do to me?" She panted while trying to catch her breath.

I stood up and grabbed my dress. "I think the question is, what have *you* done to me?" I smiled at her. Kyra gave me a tight-lipped smile.

I headed to my bathroom to shower. I didn't want to get her smell off me, but I was so used to showering right after sex. I replayed the experience as the water from my rainfall showerhead hit my face. Until that moment, I wondered if I had ever truly loved someone because if this wasn't love, I didn't know what it could be.

I walked back into the bedroom to find Kyra fast asleep. I didn't want to wake her. I wanted her to feel comfortable and realize this is where she could be relaxed. With all that she had going on, I just wanted her to have a place to get away from the world if needed. More than I wanted to be her woman, I wanted Kyra to be happy. I could tell she had the weight of the world on her shoulders.

I wanted to take some of that weight and help her know she didn't have to do everything alone.

I watched her sleep. An image of the future flashed in my head. We could be amazing together. I saw us as one of those amazing couples people admired. We could build an empire. Take the music industry and Hollywood by storm. More than anything, I believed in her dreams. I wanted her to succeed and was willing to help whenever she needed me to. I saw what we could be. I just needed her to see it too.

Kyra woke up two hours later. She looked around, trying to remember where she was. I smiled at her. She picked up her phone and jumped up.

"Shit, man, I didn't mean to fall asleep," she said while gathering all her things. "I'm late."

"It's almost one in the morning. You don't have to go, do you?" I questioned. I didn't want her to leave.

"Yeah, um, we're doing a late set. I am so sorry I fell asleep. You wore me out, woman," she smirked.

"Just give me a minute. I can drive you to wherever you need to go." I stood up.

Kyra shook his head. "I'm good. I drove here."

I watched Kyra rush to pack all her things while checking her phone every few minutes. Then finally, she ran to the door, and I followed.

"Thank you again for everything. I'll call you later." She kissed me on my forehead. I was disappointed. I wanted another one of our amazing kisses.

Just like that, she was gone. Traces of her scent lingered in my house. I wanted to feel good, but I had this lingering feeling of regret. I did so much for it to end on a low note. I decided not to focus on that. I was overall happy with the night and couldn't wait 'til she was with me again.

Chapter 14

I put the finishing touches on my invitation for my birthday event. I was excited for the first year ever because I had a romantic interest on my birthday. I had given up on dating during my birthday. The few times I was with someone on my birthday, they typically ruined it for me. So I decided years ago to do what I wanted on my birthday. That way, the only person I could blame for a bad time was myself.

Last year was my best birthday ever. I spent it in Miami at a big Comic-Con with a lot of Spartacus's cast. On my actual day, I got serenaded by one of my favorite actors from the show. I also met Tamiak from *The Last Dragon,* a dream come true. I had always wanted to ask Bruce Leroy if he could "teach me some moves."

I didn't know if anything could top Miami. My fellow nerdy friends treated me to a fantastic dinner with mojitos on South Beach. I partied, danced, and smoked hookah. It was the beginning of my decision to start doing the things that I wanted to do. Typically, I would throw an event for my birthday that usually turned out to be more work than fun. The one thing I could always rely on for my birthday was my cake. They were always themed and designed to a tee. But this year, due to work, I couldn't plan a trip as I wanted. Plus, I knew I wanted Kyra to be with me the next time I went out of town. Things had slowed down again after her birthday. I knew with the summer season, she would have a lot of gigs. There were rooftop parties, lounges, and restaurants that all wanted live music.

A new gaming bar had just opened in Memphis, and I knew it was perfect for my birthday. I planned an entire theme around old-school gaming, including a cake in the shape of the original Nintendo controller. I just wanted to hang with my friends, play all our old-school video games, and chill.

I made sure Kyra knew my birthday was coming up and informed her about my party. Communication fell short again, but I knew it was because of her gigs. I didn't want to seem needy, so I let it slide. My friends even assured me that people don't need to text or talk all day to care about someone. I was trying not to let it bother me. My birthday was in a few days, and I knew I would see her then. She promised me she was coming to the party. Even when I told her it was all right if she missed it, she assured me she would be there. I knew it was going to be a good birthday.

Kyra had already told me that her gig was early and that she would come to the party right after the event. After that, she would return to my house where we would celebrate privately. I could hardly concentrate at work. All I could think about was finally spending a birthday in the arms of someone I loved.

I was enjoying a marathon of *The Office* when my doorbell chimed. I wasn't expecting anyone, so I picked up my phone to check my ring doorbell. Kyra was standing there with her backpack in her hand.

"Hey," I said through the speaker on my phone. I watched as Kyra looked directly into the camera.

"Hey, sorry to just show up. Are you busy? Can I come in?"

"Of course," I said as I put my slippers on my feet. "I'm on my way."

I opened the door, and Kyra walked in with her backpack almost busting open with items. She seemed off, not making eye contact with me.

"I'm sorry to show up like this. I was wondering if I could take a quick shower. I got a gig and didn't have time to make it across town." Kyra shifted her weight from one foot to the other, still not making direct eye contact.

"Of course, that's not a problem. Use the shower in my bathroom."

Kyra followed me to my bedroom. I grabbed a towel set and handed it to her as she rummaged through her backpack. I noticed multiple pieces of clothing stuck in the bag. Was she working so many gigs that she didn't even have time to go home to change between them? I wanted to ask but figured it wasn't the time. As she headed to the bathroom, I returned to my living room and *The Office* marathon. Thirty minutes later, Kyra appeared fully dressed, and her wet hair pulled back in a curly ponytail.

"Babe, that shower. On God, what is that?" she said as she sat down on the couch. She started folding her worn clothes and stuffing them into her backpack. "I've never felt anything like that in my life."

"I figured you would like it," I smiled.

"Girl, I almost moved in there. I think your bathroom might be bigger than my bedroom at my apartment."

We both laughed.

Kyra gushed about the new band she had put together with a couple of friends while packing her bag. I loved listening to her talk about music. I knew the feeling. Her passion for music was the same passion I had for writing. She was concerned about growing the social media presence for the band and getting the name out there. I offered to assist. With writing, I had become pretty proficient in promoting myself, especially online. Listening to her made me want to help her in reaching her goals. I wanted her to stay, but she let me know she had to get to practice.

"Hey, so I'll still see you Saturday, right?" I asked as I walked her to the door.

"Yes, ma'am. I'm ready to play some video games." Kyra smiled. "Thank you again for letting me use that immaculate shower of yours." She gave me a quick peck on my lips before walking out of my house.

I had a special surprise for Kyra. I called her and got no answer, so I texted and asked her to swing by my house. She responded, saying she had an appointment but asked me to meet her at IHOP for breakfast. I pulled into the lot just as she was walking up. I wondered where she was walking from. Her apartment was close but not close enough to walk to. It was also misting outside. I hated to think of her walking in the rain.

"You could have asked me to pick you up," I said as we walked into the restaurant. It was empty for a morning. I knew it would look different on the weekend.

Kyra smiled. "I wasn't coming from home. I just got off the bus down the street." She pulled her hoodie off, exposing her bushy hair in a messy man bun held together by a single rubber band.

"But it's raining." I wiped some water off her hoodie. I hated seeing her in it. But the more time I spent with her, the more I realized that many of her clothes were worn out and not distressed as a fashion statement.

"Girl, I told you, I'm a nomad. It's just water. No biggie." She pointed to a waitress and smiled.

I followed Kyra to a section of the restaurant in the back. The staff greeted her by name. She spoke to all of them. She was obviously here a lot. I pulled my MacBook out and placed it on the table while Kyra proceeded to order without looking at the menu. I watched the exchange between her and the older white waitress. The waitress joked with her about her drink of choice. She knew her order already. I ordered a stack of pancakes before opening my computer.

"So, what do you have for me?" She squinted her eyes, giving me a seductive look.

"Not that," I joked, opening my computer. "So, the other day, you were talking about your band and mentioned a bunch of things you needed to get done. I hope you don't think I overreached, but I decided to take one of those things off your plate."

I turned the computer toward her. Her brow went up as she realized she was looking at a fully designed website for her band. Kyra glanced at me before focusing back on the computer. I watched as she attempted to fight the enormous smile that

was trying to appear on her face. The right side of
her mouth curled upward as she bit her bottom lip.
Kyra shook her head in amazement.

"You did this for me?" she asked as her gaze settled back on me.

I nodded. "It wasn't much. I know you mentioned it, and I can do it fairly easily, so I just put
the shell together. You can update it yourself." I
clicked the mouse to go to the admin page to show
her how to work it.

Kyra hung on to my every word as I showed
her how to work the site. She placed her hand on
my knee, rubbing it subtly. Our food arrived a few
moments later. She expressed over and over how
grateful she was to me. I was happy just seeing the
smile on her face.

"I do have one more thing for you. Now, this you
cannot keep but since I'm pretty sure you won't be
able to do anything with that dinosaur of a computer you walk around with, I've decided to let you
borrow one of mine," I said as I pulled out one of
my older laptops that I didn't use anymore.

"Are you for real?" She put her hand on her forehead. "God, why are you so good to me?"

"Because I feel you deserve it." I put my hand on
her knee. "You deserve this and so much more."

"Paige?"

We both turned our heads when we heard someone say my name. Standing a few feet in front of

me was a guy named David I hung out with during a lonely spell almost two years ago. We were in a group of plus-size women and men who liked plus-size women. I remained cordial with him but calling him a friend would be a stretch. We would speak and flirt a little when I saw him out and about, but that was it. I hadn't been that involved with the group recently, but he would hit me up from time to time. We never had sex. I couldn't get past his inability to hold a conversation without mentioning sex or how much he liked my size. I realized many of those groups were filled with people just wanting to fetishize women, and I never enjoyed that. So I only showed up from time to time. David walked closer, and his furrowed brow told me he was wondering why I was there and curious about who I was with.

"David, how are you?" I removed my hand from Kyra's knee, hoping he hadn't seen it, and stood up. We hugged each other.

"I thought that was you." David's baritone voice carried through the section. "I was like, I know that isn't Paige slumming it in Hickory Hood."

David's eyes shifted to Kyra, then back to me. I realized he was waiting on an introduction. But I knew that he really wanted an explanation.

"Oh, David, this is Kyra Preston. Kyra, this is David, an old friend," I casually replied.

David pointed at Kyra. "You look so familiar to me."

"Yeah, I feel like I've seen you before too. Do you go to Havana?" Kyra asked him.

David's eyes widened. "The band. You are in the band that plays at the cigar bar. The guitarist, right?"

"Yeah," Kyra stood up. She extended her hand to shake David's hand. "Nice to properly meet you."

A smile covered David's face. "I love you guys. Yo, ya girl here be smashing it," David sat down next to me at the table, "playing her ass off." He smiled as he turned his attention back to me. "So, what are y'all up to in this joint?"

I knew what he was up to. I wanted to tell David to mind his own business, but the last thing I wanted was my name in messy gossip in the group.

"Paige decided to take pity on the technology challenged. She is teaching me how to update my new website." Kyra smiled at me. I couldn't help but blush.

"Oh," David replied. "That makes sense. Paige is great at that stuff."

I wanted to laugh. I could hear the disappointment in his voice. He was itching to find some dirt on me. Then he could tell people we didn't work out because I was gay and not because he was dull and boring, causing me to lose interest.

"She is. I especially love how she breaks it down in small words and repeats herself over and over so that I can retain the knowledge." Kyra smiled. She was laying it on thick, and I loved it.

"That's awesome. Oh, Paige, I saw your flyer for your birthday party. I will try to make it; get my old-school game on." David motioned as if he were holding a game controller. "You owe me a round in *Call of Duty* anyway. Are you going to be at the party, Kyra?"

Kyra nodded her head. "Miss the chance to celebrate my teacher's birthday? Of course not. I'll be there with bells on." She looked at me and smiled.

The waitress called for David.

"Well, let me get out of here. I'll see you guys Saturday." David stood up. We said our goodbyes as he headed to the counter to pick up his to-go order.

"So about my birthday." I casually nudged her.

"This Saturday, your big day. I remember," she said without looking up from the computer.

"Anything special planned for after the party? Do I need anything in particular at the house or anything?" I smirked.

"Look at you trying to get some info out of me. But I'm like Fort Knox, baby. I'm not telling you anything." Kyra winked.

We finished up with everything and headed out of IHOP. The rain was starting to come down hard.

I offered Kyra a ride, but she refused it. I watched as she took off, walking in the opposite direction. I thought about following to make sure she didn't end up needing a ride after all, but I knew she wouldn't like that, so I left, hoping she didn't catch a cold due to her stubbornness.

Chapter 15

Saturday arrived. One by one, my extended group of friends and associates came to my party. The game bar was huge, with large sectionals set up, creating individual living room spaces for each group that people rented for a time to play all the gaming consoles. The games people played projected on the wall like a giant TV screen. My more nerdy friends debated on what games we were going to play first and made friendly wagers on who would win while my non-gamer friends hit the bar for libations. Even some people who didn't play games found their way to the arcade games. Some friends who didn't play console games still enjoyed a good old arcade game. I tried to focus on my event, but I couldn't concentrate because I kept looking at the front door. I was waiting to see Kyra walk in.

It was almost the end of the party, and still no Kyra. I sent her multiple texts to see where she was, but she never replied. My friends had a great time and even offered to extend my time in the living room section we rented. They bought two more hours because they were having so much fun. I, on the other hand, was not.

I was trying my best to look like I was having fun, but I knew I needed to get away before my face gave away my true feelings. So I walked to the arcade game section and began playing one of the Pac-Man machines. A few minutes into my game, Morgan walked over to me.

"So . . ."

"Yeah?" I couldn't look at her. I continued to play the game.

"Has she at least called?" I could hear the concern in her voice.

I put a smile on my face and turned to my friend. "Oh yeah, I meant to tell you earlier. She got stuck at the gig she had. It was running late. And I honestly didn't expect her to come anyway. We just hanging out, you know." I smiled, quickly turning back to the game. I pressed start and began playing again.

"I hear you, but—"

"But nothing. It's all good, Morgan. If I'm not tripping, neither should you." I forced a big smile on my face.

The night finally came to an end. I had never been so ready to get home in my life. I loved my friends, but they were not who I truly wanted to spend my birthday with. I was worried. I knew there was no way Kyra would miss my birthday on purpose. Something had to keep her held up. Maybe the lie I fed Morgan was true. It was the only thing I could think of that made sense and didn't make me feel horrible. Plus, the night wasn't over. She was supposed to come to my house anyway, so I went home, knowing she would be with me before my birthday ended.

Three hours later, I sat on my couch eating leftover cake and drinking wine. Worry was settling in. I wondered if something had happened to her. I called her phone, but it went to voicemail after two rings. I knew that meant she sent me to voicemail. Worry morphed into anger as I sent one final text.

????

There was still no reply. I needed to do something to take my mind off her. I scrolled through the hundreds of birthday greetings from my friends and fans on my Facebook page. I was furious. Not only had I not talked to her all day, but she also didn't text or even post a generic "Happy Birthday" message on Facebook. There was no excuse. Only a couple of hours were left before my birthday ended, and I had not heard from the one person I wanted to hear from more than anything.

My mind raced. What could make her forget something so important so easily? Kyra knew it was my birthday. We had just talked about it. I wanted to find a reason—something to make me believe she didn't just completely say fuck me and my birthday. But there was no reason that could explain it.

I clicked on her profile. My heart shattered when I read a post from a few minutes earlier.

Kyra: Shout out to Keisha and Brandy for being the best two women in my life. You are always there for a sista when she needs you—blessed to have them in my life.

I wanted to scream. Not only did she ignore my birthday, but she actually gave a shout-out to other women on *my* day. I was pissed. Kyra never publicly recognized me for anything that I did for her. Hell, I had just created a website for her and given her my computer. Where was my "Thank you" post?

Anger turned to self-deprecation. Thoughts flooded my mind. This was my fault. I allowed this to happen. Once again, I let someone I was romantically involved with ruin my birthday. Once again, I went over and beyond for someone who didn't care enough about me to do the bare minimum. I wasn't expecting a big gift. I knew her broke ass couldn't afford much. I wasn't expecting a gift at all. All I wanted was to spend time with her—time I so desperately desired.

Everything was making sense. I spent all these months living for the little bit of time she chose to give to me. Sporadic text messages and phone calls all blamed on her "busy schedule" was all some utter bullshit. She wasn't the only one with a busy life. I worked a full-time job and also had books to write, yet I always made time for her.

My phone rang, pulling me out of my angry moment. I picked it up, hoping it was Kyra. Instead, Loyal's name appeared on my screen.

"What's up, chica? I'm up here, but I don't see you," Loyal yelled over the loud music in the club.

"Loyal, it's over. It was over at eight," I snapped.

"Damn, I was thinking you guys would still be partying. Are you busy? I got something for you."

I was shocked. Loyal and I were cool but not cool enough that I thought he would give me something for my birthday.

"Well, I live down the street. If you want to come over, you can. I'm here, alone," I grumbled.

"Oh, OK, cool. Text me your address."

I could smell him before the moment I opened my door. One thing about Loyal was his cologne was always amazing. He walked in and immediately started looking at the book covers on my wall. He looked good as he always did. Loyal was so different from Kyra. He was very well dressed. Each outfit I ever saw him in looked brand new. He kept his head clean-shaven without any stubble. Even his beard was perfectly lined. If he stood next to Kyra, he would make her look like a homeless person.

"Damn, Paige, I didn't know you were living like this. Very nice," Loyal said as he followed me to the living room.

"Thanks. Would you like something to drink?" I said, holding up the bottle of wine I had been nursing since I got home.

He took the bottle from me and read the label. He spoke Italian perfectly. Then he picked up the empty wineglass and poured a little. He tasted it, making reference to the taste. He knew his wines. I was impressed.

"So, I got you this. It's nothing big," he said as he handed me a birthday card.

"Thank you." I opened the card. It was a *Doctor Who* birthday card with a twenty-five-dollar gift card for Cheesecake Factory. I smiled. "I can't believe you know anything about *Doctor Who*."

He frowned. "I don't, but I know you got that shit all over your desk. And they didn't have a Spartacus or Bruno Mars card, so I figured this was the next best thing."

We both laughed.

My smile quickly faded. Loyal noticed instantly and questioned why I looked so glum.

"You are my coworker. We are cool and all, but it's not like you are someone super close to me."

"Well, damn. I'd think we were pretty close," he laughed.

I wanted to smile, but I couldn't. "My point is, we are work friends. But you cared enough to give me this. Yet, the person that I'm crazy about didn't care enough even to call me on my birthday."

I held a tight smile as my eyes welled with tears. Once that first tear broke free, the rest followed in an unbroken stream. I buried my face in my hands. Not only was I heartbroken, but now, I was embarrassed as well.

I felt Loyal's strong hand grip my shoulder.

"Come on now, don't cry." Loyal wrapped his hands around my wrists. I looked up at his face. He looked genuinely concerned.

"I'm sorry. Here, you thought you were walking in to a happy person, and I'm over here crying over a guy," I sobbed.

Loyal sat at the edge of my couch. "Paige, it's obvious that you didn't take my original advice. This is still the musician, isn't it? The girl guitarist?"

I looked up in shock. He smiled.

"How did you know?"

"I mean, did you really think I wasn't going to catch those times you almost said she instead of he? Give me more credit than that."

"You surprised?" I asked as I wiped tears from my face.

"I am. I didn't know you were into girls."

"It's a long story, but I guess you can call me bisexual. A bisexual idiot who fell for someone after being warned not to. I should have listened to you."

Loyal shook his head. "I mean, this is why I told you not to get too deep. I'm not going to say she doesn't like you, but the fact that she didn't even call you on your birthday should let you know that she doesn't truly care about you the way you want her to."

I knew Loyal was right. I had to face the truth. I wasn't what I thought I was to Kyra. I made a huge mistake, and now I am suffering because of it.

"Tell me what to do. You've been in this situation before."

"What do you mean?"

"Come on, Loyal, we all know about Rayne." I looked at him. Rayne was our coworker who was gay that he hooked up with. She disappeared shortly after they ended, blaming it on moving to New York for her art career. But the word around the call center was she ran to get away from him and her feelings for him.

Loyal sat back on my couch. He took another big gulp of the wine. "Okay, since y'all know everything, I will tell you the truth. Yes, I hooked up with Rayne, and yes, it was a bad idea. She got a little too attached, and I wasn't in it for all that. We were having fun, and it got complicated. I regret it because I lost a friend. But in the end, I told her what the deal was, and she couldn't handle it. Sorta like you don't seem to be handling this thing well with this chick." Loyal finished his wine and poured another glass. "I want something stronger than this. Got any brown?"

I stood up and walked over to my bar. I held up a bottle of D'Ussé Cognac XO. Loyal clapped his hands.

"Oh shit, you got that good shit."

"I had got it to share with her, but, well, she's not here."

"Well, I will definitely take a glass or two in her place. Matter of fact, get two. It's your birthday, so let's turn up."

Loyal and I watched YouTube videos on my smart TV while laughing and talking. He told me the reason he was late for my birthday party. He was fucking a girl, and things just went a little longer than expected. I couldn't help but be entertained by his stories. Before I knew it, it was four in the morning, and we were drunk.

I stood up.

"I just wanna curse her out so bad!" I yelled as I sloppily moved around my living room.

Loyal shook his head. "That's not the way. You have every right to be angry, but yelling isn't going to get the response you want. You gotta play the game. Honestly, when she calls, act as if you don't care. You gotta let her know that she is disposable. You don't need her. Let her know it was fucked-up but dismiss it. Hang up with her quickly and act like you have something better going on. Then do *not* answer her calls or texts for at least a week, longer actually."

"You think that would work?" I asked.

Loyal finished the last of the cognac in his glass. "Trust me; it will work. But more importantly, you gotta get your feelings under control. This is not a woman to love; this is a woman to fuck and send her on her way."

"Ugh, but that's not what her ass keeps saying to me. One minute, she's making me think we have a real future together. And the next, I'm over here drunk with you. I wish she would just be honest about what she wants."

"Paige," Loyal sat up straighter on my couch, "she will *never* make you her girlfriend." His words cut me like a knife. I held in my emotions. "Enjoy her for what she is, and don't expect anything more. And if you can't do that, leave her alone."

We were both tired and drunk. I wasn't going to let him drive home, so I offered him my guest room for the night. The following day, I heard a knock on my bedroom door. I told him to open the door. Loyal walked into my bedroom looking like a million dollars while I felt like shit.

"Hey, so I'm going to get out of here. Thanks for letting me crash," he smiled.

"No problem. Let me walk you to the door."

Loyal gave me a big hug before leaving my house. I felt confident. I wasn't going to allow anyone, not even Kyra, to make me feel the way I felt that night ever again. This would be the last time I let someone to ruin my birthday.

Chapter 16

Two more days passed without any word from Kyra. I tried to remember the things Loyal told me to do, but I found it becoming harder and harder. I wanted to go off. Not only did she forget about my birthday, but she wasn't even woman enough to call me and apologize.

My breaking point came at my job. I was checking my Facebook when I saw her post a status update for the first time in days. Kyra had the time to get on Facebook but not the time to contact me. I was livid. Without thinking, I opened my text messages and sent her a text telling her I needed my computer back today. Within moments, she responded, saying she would bring it by when I got off.

I rushed home. Although pissed, I wanted to look good when I cursed her out. That plan went out the window when I saw Kyra sitting in a chair on my patio, waiting on me to arrive. I didn't speak. I opened my door and headed to my living room. She followed. I sat down in my chair. She entered the living room, opened her backpack, and set the computer down before turning to walk out the door.

"Um, wait a minute," I called out before she left the room. Kyra turned around with a frustrated look on her face. "So, are you really *not* going to talk to me at all?"

"Look, I know we need to talk, but I need to get to practice," she huffed. "I need to apologize, but we also need to talk about what I am actually apologizing for."

"What does that mean? You mean you can't give me *five* minutes?" I pleaded.

Kyra sighed as she looked at her phone. "I can't right now, but I will come back after rehearsal."

There was nothing I could do. I watched her walk out of the door. I didn't know what to think or feel. I was more confused than ever. I didn't know what she meant about what she needed to apologize for. There was only one thing that I was upset about. She had to know what it was. I was going to have to wait for answers.

I woke up on my couch. I wasn't sure when I fell asleep. It was dark outside. I grabbed my phone. It was almost eleven, and I had no missed calls or texts from Kyra. I sent her a text to find out where she was.

Kyra: Can't make it. Will have to be another day.

That was it. I couldn't take anymore. She stood me up for the last time. I was not about to be the girl waiting around for a girl who couldn't make time for me. I thought about what Loyal told me to do. I sent a reply.

Paige: Whatever, Kyra.

I wanted to throw my phone across the room. I couldn't believe how she was acting. I let out a frustrated grunt just as my text message notification rang. I picked up my phone to see a text from her.

Kyra: See, this is the type of shit I'm not dealing with. You know what? No need to talk. Let's just go our separate ways.

My hands were shaking. I felt the room spinning. I reread the message. She just ended things with me over a text message? My heart was racing. There were so many things I expected. I expected to yell and for her to apologize. I expected some weak excuse about why she didn't show up. But never in a million years did I expect Kyra to end things.

Paige: Are you kidding me right now? All I wanted to do was talk, and you go to this extreme? What did I do to deserve that? This is fucked-up, Kyra. Completely fucked-up.

I sat waiting on a response. Finally, one came.

Kyra: Look, it was real, but I got too much going on. I can't deal with you. It is what it is.

I gasped for air. I felt like my body was closing down on me. She was serious. Kyra really was trying to leave me alone. I felt helpless and scared. I was mad, but I couldn't fathom not having her in my life.

Paige: Kyra, don't do this. It's not that serious. Don't take this to such an extreme.

I didn't care about my birthday anymore. I didn't care about all the disappearing acts or the sporadic texting. All I cared about was losing Kyra. She was ending us before we even began. I didn't want that. I couldn't accept it. I was going to wait on her to text me back. This couldn't really be ending this way. I sat there, waiting on a text.

A text that never came.

Chapter 17

I couldn't cry anymore. I was numb. I couldn't feel a single feeling at all. Life became nothing more than work and home. I couldn't write. I didn't want to do anything besides be alone. Before I knew it, a month had passed, and I was still numb. I wondered if I would ever feel anything again.

Everything reminded me of her. Traces of Kyra covered every corner of my home. I couldn't sleep in my bed because I wanted her arms around me. My living room was just as difficult to be in. Flashbacks of us, writing, me listening to her play her acoustic guitar while explaining progressions and things I didn't quite understand. I couldn't listen to any of the music that she put me on to or that I introduced her to. I was waiting on the day that I snapped out of it. I didn't want to feel this way anymore.

Finally, the day came when I woke up and didn't care. Overnight, it felt like a weight had been lifted off my shoulders. I started to feel again. I treated myself to a couple of movies and even allowed my friends to come over and hang out. It was taking time, but slowly, Kyra was leaving my heart.

I received a call from a guy friend name Niko. He was excited about being featured at the poetry night and wanted me to come. I panicked. I hadn't been to The Lounge in a while, especially not since Kyra ended things. I knew Kyra would be there, and I didn't know if I was ready to face her yet. I was coming up on the end of the second month of not talking to her and knew I would have to face my fears at some point. At least my friends would be there with me.

I sat outside The Lounge, trying to get the nerve up to go in. I called my friends, all of whom had various reasons why they couldn't make it after all. Just as I was getting ready to leave, Niko walked up to my car, excited to see me there. I knew it was now or never.

I could feel Kyra's presence as I walked up to the building. I walked in and immediately made eye contact with her. She looked at me, winked, and continued to play. I felt my heart drop. I couldn't watch her play, so I headed to the bar. I would need to drink a lot to get through this night.

"What can I get you?" the woman behind the bar asked me. She was new and looked vastly different from the regular bartenders. They tended to have extremely attractive bartenders and servers. This girl looked frumpy and plain. She was plus-sized, and unlike the other bartenders who typically dressed nicely, she wore baggy jeans and a basic button-down shirt.

"Something strong," I said as I sat on the bar stool.

"Oh, you sound like my girlfriend," She smiled while pouring vodka. "You should like this. I know Kyra does." She poured a few more things together before topping it with orange juice.

My eyes widened. I thought I was losing my mind. There was no way she said her girlfriend was Kyra.

"Kyra, the guitarist?" I questioned as I took a sip of the drink.

She nodded her head. "Yeah. Do you know her?"

I shrugged my shoulders. "Only from the band's Facebook page," I lied. I needed more information.

"Oh yeah, I swear I would not be here if it weren't for her. They making us work the bar now since their bartenders didn't come in. I just got off work and had to come to work this bar. And it's slow tonight. I gotta drink myself," she laughed.

"I feel ya. I just got off work too." I forced a smile. "I better slow down on this drink before I can't make it home."

"Girl, I know, right? I already told Kyra she's driving home 'cause I am so going to sleep in the car." She put her hand up to give me a high five.

Home. They live together, I thought to myself. There was no way Kyra met a girl and moved in with her in less than two months. All the puzzle pieces finally fit together. Now I understood why she could never spend the night and why she disappeared so much. I wanted to cry, but I wasn't going to give her the satisfaction. So instead, I placed a couple of dollars in the tip jar and headed to Niko's table.

I sat there in a daze. So many things ran through my mind. I wanted answers. I wanted to know was all of it a lie. Was she with the frumpy bartender the entire time we were together? My evil side wanted to walk up and blow up Kyra's spot. Let Little Miss Frumpy know precisely who she's in a relationship with. But the calculated Cancer in me knew that wouldn't do anything but cause a scene, and I did have a career I had to think about. So I sat there, fuming, cutting my eyes at Kyra, who was oblivious to my evil gaze.

I finally refused to look at her. Instead, I focused on my phone, scrolling up and down my Facebook and Instagram timelines. I took time to send texts to my friends just to look busy. Once I ran out of things to do, I headed to *The Shade Room* to read articles, anything to not look at Kyra. Her guitar solos were the hardest for me. I was the moth to the flame. Finally, I broke, shifting my eyes in her direction.

But it was different. As if my rose-colored glasses had finally come off, I didn't see her as perfect any longer. I noticed her flaws. She had on those same worn-out pants and hoodie with holes in it that I hated. Her hair looked like it hadn't been combed in weeks. But she still was a master on guitar, and with every strum, I felt my heart skip a beat.

"What's up, chick?"

I felt a tap on my shoulder. I turned as Morgan sat down next to me.

"Oh my God, thank you for coming." I squeezed her hand. "Someone to help me get through this hell."

"I can't believe you are even here," she said while sipping her drink. "I hope you haven't been losing it."

I told her about the interaction with the bartender. I quickly noticed that her face didn't change. It was apparent she knew about the woman.

"So, we felt they were involved somehow, but I didn't think they were official." Morgan glanced over at the girl. "I mean, look at her. She looks busted all the time."

"Why didn't you tell me?" I tried to remain calm.

"I honestly didn't think they were an actual couple. They are never affectionate. Plus, I figured you knew what you were dealing with. Paige, Kyra is a musician, and she's given you multiple signs that she ain't shit. So I figured you knew how to deal with an 'ain't shit nigglet.'" Morgan sipped her drink, completely ignoring my mortified face.

She was right. The signs were there. I just chose to ignore them because of our connection. I wondered if *any* of it was true . . . telling me how she wanted to settle down and that she could see us together . . . Was it all just a game? But what was the purpose of this twisted game? I knew from the moment she sent the first message that I was interested. Did she not know she could've had me without the lies?

The show ended, and the crowd began to disburse. I sat listening to Morgan's girlfriend talking to another artist about an event she was planning. I acted interested in the conversation and kept eye contact with them. I couldn't shift my eyes. If I did, I knew *exactly* where they would end up.

Morgan and her girlfriend were finishing up their conversation. I began gathering my things and stood up from the booth. I successfully made it through the evening without incident. I just needed to make it to my car, and I could call the night a success. I walked out of the building—only to run directly into Kyra. We stared at each other for a moment.

"Yo, so, I finally finished *Spartacus*," She broke the silence while shaking her head. "I can't believe it ended like that."

Is this nigga really talking about Spartacus?
I thought to myself while listening to her go on
about the final episode. She acted as if she hadn't
ripped my heart out of my chest.

"Yeah, I gotta go," I said, cutting her off during
her *Spartacus* spiel.

"It was wonderful seeing you, Paige Writes,"
Kyra responded as she placed her hand on my
shoulder.

I felt a surge of energy pulling through my arm,
radiating through my entire body. I needed to get
away from her before I couldn't control myself
anymore. Even after finding out about her girlfriend, Kyra could still render me helpless in her
presence. The old jeans, her uncombed hair, none
of it mattered. I wanted Kyra's arms around me,
but I refused to let her know. Instead, I kept my
straight-faced expression. I wasn't going to give
her the satisfaction of knowing she still affected
me.

"What's up, Kyra?" Morgan said as she walked
out of the building, instantly saving me from myself.

"Magnificent Morgan," Kyra's voice echoed
down the street. She wrapped her arms around
Morgan, giving her a huge hug. Morgan looked
genuinely confused. "What's going on, girl?"

"Nothing much," Morgan turned toward me.
"You ready to go?"

I nodded. Kyra said goodbye to both of us. Morgan answered for me. I simply looked at her. Kyra's forehead wrinkled in confusion as if she didn't understand why I was acting so unbothered. I turned and walked away, hoping that look of confusion stayed on her face.

Morgan turned to make sure Kyra was in the building. Then she grabbed me by my arm and pulled me close.

"Tea to spill," she whispered. "So, yeah, just found out that is her chick, but it seems as if she knows Kyra ain't shit. Someone just told me that a few weeks ago, they got into a huge argument outside of Minglewood. Kyra was stupid drunk and was wailing on her about messing with other women. Seems that Piko and Trey from the band had to pull them apart and everything. Girl, Kyra ain't shit, and you dodged a bullet."

We stopped at my car. "Why would she stay with Kyra then?" I questioned. Why would *anyone* stay in a relationship with someone they knew was cheating?

"Girl, who knows? Kyra is talented. Maybe her girl thinks if she's there for her in the beginning, if Kyra ever gets big, she'll get the ring. People like Kyra you have to deal with accordingly. Fuck her and send her on her merry way." Morgan pulled her phone out and started tapping away on it. Loyal's voice echoed the same sentiments.

I said my goodbyes to Morgan, somehow hiding the way I was truly feeling. I had so many emotions running through me, but the overwhelming feeling was just disappointment. I was disappointed in Kyra for playing me and disappointed in myself for allowing it to happen. I had been through this enough times to know better, but here I was, back in a very familiar boat.

I thought about everything Morgan and Loyal had said on my drive home. Even though I was deeply hurt, it was apparent that I still cared about Kyra. I wanted to think of all the bad regarding her, but I couldn't stop thinking about our good times. My mind focused on our wonderful conversations and the last time we were intimate. I knew I needed to cut myself off from her completely. I couldn't be around her anymore, not anywhere. I made a mental note that it would be my last time going to an event where I knew she would be for a very long time.

I finally made it home, quickly uncorking my bottle of wine and pouring a nightcap. The night replayed in my mind. Kyra has a girlfriend, and it seems to be a toxic relationship. I felt the frumpy girl had to be stupid for dealing with Kyra, but she had the title. So, if she were stupid, that made me certifiably insane for still caring about her at all.

Chapter 18

I tried to focus at work, but it just wasn't happening. I couldn't get the previous night out of my head. Finally, I turned around in my chair and looked at my coworkers.

"Would you ever date someone who you know has someone else?" I asked. My question caused Tara and Shantel's heads to turn immediately.

"Be a side piece? Hell no." Shantel frowned.

"I did, but I didn't know I was the side piece. It was actually rather good until I found out." Tara folded her arms.

"But you didn't know. That's way different than being a willing participant. I could never be a willing side piece." Shantel shook her head. "What kind of life is that?"

"Yeah, but at the same time, sometimes, side pieces get treated just as good, or even better than the wifey. I know, in my case, the dude did everything for me. He did so much for me that I didn't even know I was a side piece until I found something in his phone. If I had never looked, I would have been blissfully happy. This was before I found my wife."

I pointed at Tara. "See, this is what I am talking about. These days, so many people cheat anyway. Wouldn't it be easier just to know already?"

"My man doesn't cheat," Shantel proudly exclaimed.

"Neither does my wife." Tara held her head high.

"OK, so in your cases, your mates don't cheat. But we all know that it happens, and a lot. Recently, I have been thinking about the simplicity of being a side chick. You don't have the drama of wondering what your mate is doing. You get all the perks and let the wifey deal with the bullshit. In reality, it sounds ideal," I added.

"What are you hens talking about?" Loyal walked up with his usual cup of coffee in hand.

"The perks of being a side chick," I said.

He nodded his head. "It is a great thing . . . when done right." Loyal took his usual seat at the empty desk.

"You would say that. You're a whore." Shantel wrinkled her nose at him.

"I'm not a whore. I am just single and doing what single people do. So why are you even thinking about side chicks?"

I informed them of the night before. While Tara and Shantel seemed utterly disgusted by the revelation, Loyal sat with a crooked smile on his face. I looked at him, and he was staring directly at me.

"What, Loyal?" I snapped.

He continued to smirk as he stood up. "I'm not going to tell you I told you so, but . . . I told you so." He winked before walking back to his desk.

"Paige, if you want this guy in your life, go ahead and be a side chick. Just make sure you lock down your heart. You can't love a man who is obviously incapable of truly loving a person back," Shantel said before turning around to answer a phone call. I was starting to feel bad that Shantel didn't know the truth. She was the only one who didn't realize Kyra was a woman.

I didn't understand the way I was feeling. I didn't think I had love for Kyra anymore. She had ruined that. I didn't care about the sex. I missed our time together. I missed the friendship. I missed the way she pushed me in my writing and the way I pushed her back. I wanted that back more than anything.

An hour later, Loyal approached me at my desk. He pulled the empty chair up to my desk, leaned in, and whispered, "I know what you're thinking about doing. Stop it."

I looked at him as he stood up, putting the chair back before walking away. He shot me one final glance before disappearing. I knew what that glance meant. He didn't believe I could be with Kyra knowing she was with someone. I wondered if he was right. But something in me wanted to try at least.

Chapter 19

After the long day at work, I just wanted to relax. I needed a release. I put in a video game and began driving around recklessly in my stolen car on *Grand Theft Auto*. Suddenly, someone knocked loudly on my door, which pulled me out of my life of crime in my video game. I had done some emotional shopping on Amazon and figured more boxes were arriving. I walked to the door and peeped through the peephole—then froze. Kyra's face was staring back.

"You know I could hear you walk up, right, Paige?" She looked into the peephole.

I unlocked the door and opened it. Kyra stood there, hair in a messy ponytail in one of her usual raggedy pairs of pants. She smiled; her dimple appeared on her right cheek. I noticed some scratches on her neck. She had a big duffle bag sitting next to her on the floor.

"Can I come in?"

I contemplated saying no. She didn't call or text. She just appeared at my door. I had every right to tell her she couldn't come in. I could lie and tell her that I had company coming over and she had to leave.

Instead, I pushed the door back, allowing her to enter.

We sat silently in the living room. Kyra wouldn't take her eyes off me. Finally, I picked up my controller and started my game. After a few moments of me ignoring her, Kyra walked over, took my remote, and turned off my game.

"All right, I totally deserve the treatment you are giving. But can you please look at me so I can apologize?"

I put down the controller. Kyra walked back and sat in my chair.

"Kyra, why are you here?"

"I didn't handle things well before. I just wanted to let you know I did things wrong," she casually replied without taking her eyes off me.

I felt my legs trembling. My mind was blank. All the things I prepared in my mind to say to her had vanished from my memory. Kyra sat there, her usual scruffy look with her hair hanging down on her shoulders, giving me her personal type of apology. I was torn. Half of me wanted nothing more than to forgive her and feel her arms around me. But the other half knew that the apology wasn't genuine. It seemed desperate, if anything. I couldn't allow her to come back into my life so quickly.

"Kyra, you have no idea how much you hurt me. The way you handled things was not just wrong. It was completely fucked up. I did nothing to deserve that treatment." I held my hands together, rubbing my palms.

"I know. I fucked up, Paige," Kyra yelled as she stood up and began pacing the floor. "You have no idea how much I have been going through. The way you were, you were on level ten from the get-go. I just couldn't deal with your disappointment on top of everything else I have going on."

"I have no idea what you are going through because you won't let me in. Kyra, all I've done is be on your schedule. Try to just be there for you when you needed me. I thought we had developed a real connection, a friendship. But after one issue, you snatch that away from me and disappear. Do you have any idea how much that hurt?"

I felt the emotional side taking over my rational side. My whole body was shaking. My voice cracked as tears started to fall from my eyes. I didn't want this. I didn't want to cry in front of her.

Kyra stood frozen in her place. She turned her face from me for a moment. I could see more scratches on the side of her face and neck.

"What happened to you?" I tried to touch her face, but she pulled away.

Kyra paced the floor before walking back up to me. Then she fell to her knees and wrapped her arms around me. She put her head in my lap. I sat still, not knowing what to do. Kyra sobbed. I was confused and worried. I wanted to help her, but I didn't know how to. So I just sat there and let her sob while I rubbed her hair.

"I am sorry, Paige. The last thing in the world I wanted to do was hurt you. This is why I tried to stay away. I don't want to see you cry, especially because of me," she whispered in my ear as she held on to me.

My brain was screaming at me to let her go. But I just couldn't make myself do it. She felt so good, but there was something else, something very different. I didn't have the same feeling I usually have with her arms around me. Kyra's arms no longer felt safe. I pulled away and wiped the tears from my eyes.

"Why are you here, Kyra? You completely stood me up on my fucking birthday. And oh, I know all about your girlfriend. You have a whole girlfriend!" I stood up and folded my arms.

Kyra stood up. She took a few steps back. "I miss you, Paige. I miss your friendship. I don't want you to hate me. I want us to be friends."

I wanted to scream. She didn't deny having a girlfriend. She just chose not to respond to anything I said. I was over this.

"Why didn't you tell me about your girlfriend, Kyra? Do you know how it felt to hear that from her that night? I felt like someone knocked the wind out of me," I yelled as I sat back on my couch. Confusion covered her face. Before she could lie, I responded. "I met her, the bartender. She was very chatty."

Kyra shook her head. "Yeah, well, can't believe everything you're told." She sounded slightly annoyed.

A cool sensation swept through my body. I wasn't sad, upset, or angry. I really didn't feel anything at all. I thought about my conversation with my coworkers and relationships in my past. I was always the faithful one, the girl who was loyal to a fault. This never worked for me. There was always another woman lurking in the background who didn't give a damn about me or my relationship. They always seemed to end up on top.

"So, are you denying that she's your girlfriend? Just be honest with me for once." My voice trembled.

Kyra was not relationship material. That much I had figured out. She had way too many issues. I had dated my fair share of struggling individuals and had outgrown that long ago. No matter how much I cared about Kyra, the truth was, she was a broke-ass, cheating musician with nothing more to offer than amazing conversation, fun times, and sex.

She sat silently, staring at me as if she were trying to read my mind. Her stare was starting to make me uncomfortable. So, finally, I stood up and walked over to my windows.

"Kyra, the funny thing is, you know you never had to lie. You had me from day one. You never had to try to get me. You didn't need to fill my head with bullshit you knew you wouldn't live up to. You never had to lie to me, and it sucks that you felt you needed to," I said.

Kyra sat back down. She let out a laugh and shook her head. "Crazy thing is you believe that."

"What?"

She started pacing the floor, shaking her head before stopping and looking directly in my eyes. "You believe that I set out to lie to you. Paige, everything I said I meant. I do want to settle down. I think you are an amazing woman, and I can see myself with you. But that doesn't negate the fact that my life took a major turn left, and I fucked up everything I thought I wanted."

"Well, I guess that doesn't matter now." I shrugged my shoulders.

"So, are you saying you don't want to be friends?"

It was as if a light had gone off in my head. I didn't want to be her girlfriend anymore, but I didn't want to lose what we had before. Her girlfriend could deal with her fucked-up ways. Miss Frumpy could be the one who worried about where

Kyra was and who she was with. She could take care of Kyra and be that support she needed, while I could have her for the things that I wanted to deal with. It suddenly all made sense to me.

I shook my head. "Not completely. I think I want to be your side chick."

Kyra's head tilted to the side. She opened her mouth, but nothing came out. Finally, she laughed and shook her head. "What, woman?"

"Kyra, when you came into my life, I was not looking for anything serious. You fed me all that stuff and made me want the possibility. But when you left, I realized that relationships are for the birds. I am in a place where I want to have fun, and I want that fun to be with you. I don't want to be your girlfriend. But I don't want to stop everything that we started."

Kyra's brow wrinkled. "So, you just want the D?"

We both laughed.

"I mean, I'm open to it, but as I said, sex was never what was overly important to me."

"Ah, that's right. You didn't like my sex." She pressed her lips closely together. "I forgot about that."

"Stop it. I've enjoyed it a lot the last few times. But seriously, I love spending time with you. Not just sexually. I don't want to give that up."

Kyra jumped up and joined me on the couch. She took her hand and placed it on my face. Then she turned my head to hers and looked into my eyes.

"Baby, listen to me when I say this. You are so much more than just some random side chick. I can never think of you that way. You have no idea how much I care about you. I'm ending something, and if you just stick by me for a little while, I promise things will be what you deserve."

Kyra stared at me with a longing I had only dreamed about seeing again. I bit my lip as I stared at her. The edge of my mouth curled upward as I held on to her shirt. I felt the seductress inside of me trying to take over. I decided not to fight her.

"See, this is something you have been denying yourself because you chose to leave me alone," I said as I grabbed her hand and led her to my bedroom. My huntress was fighting for power, a power I was usually denied when dealing with the people in my past. I was always the submissive one, giving my people whatever they wanted. But this time, I was taking the lead. It felt liberating, and Kyra followed suit.

I pulled my pants down and crawled onto the bed. Kyra pulled her T-shirt over her head. She kissed me. I let the taste of her tongue ignite the fire burning in me. I pushed her head down between my legs. I didn't want her strap. I wanted her mouth. And she devoured me with confidence and skill. I wasn't used to this feeling, a desire that had been ignored for far too long. But as much as I wanted Kyra to love it, I was getting pure satisfaction from the power of being in control. From the moans escaping her mouth, I knew she was enjoying pleasing me.

When Kyra put on her strap, we were completely in sync. Sex was at a high that we had never experienced together. As her body tensed and she alerted me of the orgasm she knew was on the horizon, I wanted more. I flipped Kyra over and straddled on top of her. I moved my body in circles, the dick deep inside, hitting all my spots. I had denied myself the pleasure I deserved for so long that my body would not allow me to return to the old ways.

I was going to have to keep Kyra around, at least until I found someone else to take her place. I was going to close off my heart and take her for exactly what she was. Kyra wasn't relationship material; she was fun material. I never had someone around just for entertainment purposes. For most of my life, I didn't think there was a way to enjoy someone without having feelings for them.

Deep down, I knew it was wrong. Kyra had a girlfriend, and she still hadn't explained their situation. And although the idea of being the other woman stung, it didn't seem to matter as much as losing the euphoric sensation my body was currently feeling. I deserved this, and I was finally going to give myself *exactly* what I deserved.

Chapter 20

The life of a side piece was working better than I had imagined. The things I used to worry about with Kyra were gone. I didn't care what she did when she was away from me. The moment I stopped caring, things took a major turn. I saw her more often. I would come home from work and have her sitting on my step, her duffle bag and backpack in tow.

I enjoyed every moment we spent together. I never knew what I was going to get from day to day. One day, she would show up only to spend our time discussing various topics, from politics to relationships. We debated everything from hot topics to politics and art. Other times, we would watch movies or just be completely silly together. But sometimes, she came in with one thing on her mind. I didn't mind because I loved the feeling I got when I pleased her.

I felt completely comfortable around Kyra again. I didn't need to stay dressed in uncomfortable clothes to impress her anymore. She accepted me for who I was, and my size didn't matter to her. This only made me want her more. She wouldn't let me go down on her but loved when I sucked her strap and allowed her to use it on any part of my body she wanted. She called me her "Little Freak," and I loved it.

"Paige, you can't keep giving me all this phenomenal sex," Kyra panted as she plopped down on my sofa next to me after another round of me riding her while watching Netflix.

"What's wrong?" I asked.

Kyra turned her head to me. I watched her eyes roam down to my body while her right hand crept up my thigh toward my chest. She rubbed my hard nipple between her thumb and index finger.

"I don't want to do anything but be here with you," she whispered as her tongue grazed my nipple.

I could feel my body betraying me again. I was ready for whatever she was about to give me.

No words were spoken. Kyra stood up and held out her hand. I placed my hand in hers as I stood up. Then I followed her to my bedroom. The bed was still messy from our last session.

Kyra's arm wrapped around me, pulling me in close to her. Her lips pressed against mine. We had kissed a million times, but this was different. There was a spark, an undeniable connection on a deeper level than any of our kisses before. She slowly pulled my dress over my head. I allowed her to. I didn't care about my size with her.

"Beautiful," she breathed in a voice deeper than usual. Kyra kissed my neck, sliding down my chest until wetness from her mouth covered my right nipple. A breeze hit me, sending chills down my body, making my nipples harder than they already were. Kyra's hand disappeared between my legs. I closed my eyes as her finger slid inside me. I opened my eyes as she pulled it back out. A wicked grin appeared on her face.

"Looks like you want me too," she smiled.

I was too aroused to answer. I wanted her fingers back inside me.

I watched as she undressed. She looked at me. "Babe, what do you use to please yourself?"

I pointed at a blue tin lunch box that looked like the TARDIS from *Doctor Who*. I hid my toy in it because none of my friends cared anything about my geeky obsession. She laughed as she picked up the lunch box.

"Seriously?" she joked. "Well, it's supposed to be bigger on the inside."

I couldn't help but laugh. We were just Kyra and Paige, two nerds in my bed.

Kyra pulled my turquoise rose out of the box. She turned it on low as she made her way on top of me. Then she pressed the top of the rose against my clit. The vibrations echoed throughout my body as she pressed it against me, causing waves to vibrate through my body. Kyra leaned in, sucking my left breast while her right hand worked the rose's magic on me. My legs trembled. I grabbed her arm and held her tightly. Next, I opened my mouth, but nothing came out. I couldn't speak. All I could do was tremble and hold on to her.

"Tell me you want it," Kyra demanded. Even without raising her voice, I knew I needed to obey.

"I want you." My voice cracked as I forced the words out.

"Tell me."

"I want you—please." I quivered.

Kyra pulled my legs up, resting them on her chest. I closed my eyes and braced myself for whatever was coming next. I felt the head of her strap press against me as she slowly entered me. My body tensed from the pleasurable pain

"Relax, baby. I won't hurt you," she reassured me.

I nodded. I trusted her with every part of me. I let go, allowing my body to relax as she went deeper. Kyra took the rose, allowing it to rub against my nipples. The sensation caused my entire body to tremble. Quickly, the pain evaporated, and passion filled me with each thrust. My nails dug into her arm, causing Kyra to let out a low growl. My lips parted as soft moans turned into loud screams for more. My body didn't belong to me anymore. An unfamiliar wave rushed through my body, causing me to cry for her. My body tensed as I spasmed, hitting the bed repeatedly with my hand. I couldn't take this. I needed out.

I tried to scoot my body back, but Kyra grabbed me. She gripped around my ass, pulling me closer. Her thrust grew faster. She held my legs as she pumped faster and harder than ever. I needed to get away. I didn't know what was happening to my body. My belly felt like it was filled with fire. I couldn't breathe. I hit her shoulder, trying to get her to stop, but she wouldn't. Kyra growled as she thrust hard and wild. Suddenly, a giant ball of pleasure exploded from me just as she let out a loud moan before pounding an even deeper thrust inside me.

Finally, Kyra dropped the rose. She stopped moving, just letting her man rest inside of me. I struggled to catch my breath as tears fell from my eyes. My body was still shaking. Why wouldn't it stop shaking?

Kyra slowly pulled out of me. She placed my legs on the bed. I felt wetness on my thighs. My bed was soaking wet. Breathing hard, Kyra collapsed next to me on the bed. She didn't move. I couldn't move. We lay there in the soaked sheets. Finally, she rested her leg on my thigh. I turned to my side, placing my right leg on her. Kyra put her arm under my head.

"Fuck," she panted as more obscenities came out of her mouth. "What a fucking waste."

"Huh?" I questioned, finally breathing regularly.

"You, all these years, you wasted. You are a force of nature," she said before planting a kiss on my forehead.

We lay there for a few moments. Finally, Kyra wrapped her arm around me, pulling me close to her. Then she kissed me on the nape of my neck.

"Paige Writes," her raspy voice whispered.

"Yes, Kyra Strums?" I smiled.

"I love you."

I froze. I couldn't believe what I had just heard. I turned over to her.

"What did you say?" I asked.

Her deep dimples appeared. In her thick accent, she replied. "Gurl, you heard me."

I lay there in disbelief as a huge smile covered my face. I didn't know what had changed in her, but I welcomed it with open arms. She was finally mine.

"I love you too."

Chapter 21

The loud blaring of Bruno Mars in my ear startled me. I woke up, my heart racing from the
surprise ring. I grabbed my phone. It was three in
the morning, and an unknown number was calling
me. I wanted to ignore it, but something told me to
answer it.

"Hello," I said while clearing my throat.

"You have a collect phone call from—"

"Kyra." Her voice echoed after the recording.

"An inmate in the Shelby County Jail. To accept
this call, press one." The recording stopped.

I felt like my heart would jump right out of my
chest. I quickly pressed one on my cell phone and
waited on the call to connect.

"Hello." Kyra's sullen voice filled my ear.

I sat up in my bed. "Kyra, what's going on?"

"I only have three minutes. I need you to do
something for me, babe."

"Anything. What's up?" I said as I grabbed my
iPad for her instructions.

I typed as Kyra gave me instructions to contact her bail bondsman. I had so many questions but knew I couldn't get any of them answered in the minute we had left on the phone.

"Are you all right?" she asked.

"I'm fine, but I'm worried about you. Kyra, what happened?" I questioned.

She sighed. "I promise to tell you everything when I get out of here. Thank you, love, for taking care of this for me." But before she could finish, the phone disconnected.

I jumped into action. I called Kyra's bondsman and let him know what was going on. He let me know that Kyra's bond information wasn't in the system yet, but he would call me as soon as he learned more. I hung up the phone and lay back down in my bed. I was restless. Questions flooded my mind. Why was she in jail? How long had she been there?

A lightbulb went off in my mind. Why did she call me first? I knew she had told me she loved me, but I didn't think we had made it to "bail me out of jail" status yet. But more importantly, why was she in jail in the first place? Did she finally get caught with all the weed she carried around? Then I remembered there was an easy way to find out at least why she was locked up. I picked up my computer and typed "Who's in Jail in Memphis, TN?" on Google. Next, I typed in Kyra's name and birthday. My lip dropped as her mugshot appeared with her charge written under it: domestic assault with bodily harm.

Various scenarios played out in my head. Had Miss Frumpy found out about me, and they got into it? Did she tell her that she was in love with me and leaving her for me? Since she called me to bond her out, I could only guess it had to do with her leaving. But what could have possibly happened that led to a fight? I knew it had to be something extreme. I couldn't imagine Kyra hitting a woman.

Since we started messing around, many reports were circulating about the bartender. Whenever Morgan found out something new, she quickly called me to spill the tea. Morgan informed me about more than one drunken outburst Kyra had at a couple of gigs. Those stories didn't help the way I saw her. I hadn't told Morgan that I was messing with Kyra again. I hadn't talked about Kyra at all with my friends. I knew their reactions, and I didn't want anyone raining on my blissfully erotic parade. I didn't feel sorry for her girlfriend at all. She knew Kyra wasn't faithful, yet she continued dealing with her. Yeah, she was nice the time I met her, but, oh well, she wasn't my concern. I was having fun with the woman I loved, and I wasn't going to end it anytime soon. I knew what Kyra and I were. We were in an open relationship, and I was all right with that.

I was worried, but I knew there was nothing I could do about it right now. I would get answers from Kyra when she got out. Right now, I just had to wait. I finally drifted back to sleep . . . only for my phone to wake me up again a few hours later. The deep voice of Howard, the bondsman, blasted through my speaker.

"So, Kyra's bond is three thousand, which means we need three hundred to get her out. Are you posting her bail?" he asked.

"Yeah, I can pay it. What do I have to do?" my voice cracked.

"Well, I'll take a payment over the phone for her. Now, tell Kyra she needs to come in and see me as soon as she gets out to sign the paperwork. But remember, she must make her court date. If she doesn't, you are on the hook for this money," he said sternly.

I paused. The idea of someone coming after me for money wasn't sitting right with me. This wasn't my responsibility. I wasn't Kyra's actual girlfriend or family. I was just her side chick. Just as I was ready to say no, another thought came into my mind. She called *me*. Kyra knew my number by heart, and I was the one she called. She trusted me enough to be the one to help her. I knew if I didn't do it today, she would spend Thanksgiving in jail. I didn't want that for her. I cared about her too much to let that happen. Plus, this last month had been incredible, and she told me she loved me. I had to help her. I told Howard I would take care of it. I gave him the credit card number I had stored in my memory.

"All right, I'll take care of everything else. Ms. Paige, let Kyra know she needs to call me when she gets out. Oh, and also make sure she knows to stay away from that woman. This can't keep happening," he warned.

"Will do. Thank you."

I missed the majority of the rest of the conversation because I was stuck on his other words. *This can't keep happening.* So, this wasn't the first time this had happened.

My mind went back to the first time she came to my house. She told me then she had been in jail for a "civil thing." Was *this* the civil issue? This was not an isolated incident. They obviously fought enough that he felt the need to say that to me. I swallowed a knot that was forming in my throat. How could she explain fighting with her girlfriend more than once? And more importantly, why would Kyra stay with someone she had such a volatile relationship with? Things were not adding up. I needed answers.

"Well, Kyra will be out in a few hours. Also, tell her not to go to that woman's house. If Kyra gets arrested again for this, I don't know if bail will be an option." Howard reiterated.

"I'll make sure she knows." I was over this conversation. It was starting to feel like Howard was trying to warn me instead of informing me.

I hung up. I was restless, unable to go back to sleep. I wanted to call one of my friends but remembered they had no idea I was even dealing with Kyra anymore. Plus, telling them that I bailed her out of jail would lead to judgments I didn't want to hear. I knew there was nothing I could do, and driving myself crazy with worry wasn't helping me either. But Kyra would be out soon, and I would be able to get the answers that I needed.

Around ten in the morning, I heard the knock on my door. I opened the door to see Kyra leaning against my wall. She looked worn out, which made sense considering her situation. She had a deep gash on the side of her face. She walked in and headed straight to my bedroom.

I grabbed my first aid kit and walked into the bedroom. Kyra had quickly pulled her clothes off and made herself comfortable in my bed. She hadn't spoken a single word. I knew she probably didn't want to talk right then.

"Do you want something for that cut?" I didn't know why I was so nervous, but I was.

"I just want to get some sleep. Can you let me do that without bothering me, please?" Kyra turned her back to me.

I was offended but tried to keep my cool. She walked into my house as if she owned the place, demanding that I not bother her. I wanted to remain calm, but my emotions took over.

"Was I a bother at two in the fucking morning when you called me to bail your ass out from your fight with your damn girlfriend?" I threw the first aid kit on the bed. "Fix your own fucking face."

I stormed out of the room. I could hear her getting out of the bed to follow me. I sat down on my couch and turned on my television. Kyra stormed into the room after me.

"Damn, Paige, I just got out of jail, and you wanna start in on me. I already know you gon' ask me a million fucking questions. Shit, can a nigga get some fucking rest first? Damn." Kyra hit the wall.

She was scaring me, but I refused to show her I was scared. Instead, I just looked at her as she stood in her spot, fuming.

"Your bail bondsman said to contact him as soon as you get out. Oh, he also said don't go back to your girlfriend's house, or you probably won't get bond again since this seems to be a repeat thing for you." I folded my arms and waited for her response.

Kyra took a deep breath. She walked over and sat next to me. She placed her hand on my knee. Her anger instantly disappeared.

"I'm sorry. I appreciate you more than you can ever imagine. I will pay you back every penny, I promise. But please, baby, can I get some sleep? I've been up for so long. I just need a couple of hours."

I didn't respond. I sat there as she stood up, making sure to give me a forehead kiss before heading back to my bedroom. I knew this wasn't over, but I wouldn't know anything until she rested.

Chapter 22

While Kyra slept, I continued to prepare for my upcoming trip. My best friend and I had been preparing for a trip to Dubai and Abu Dhabi for months. We were now less than a week away, and I was so consumed with Kyra that I hadn't finished anything. My large rolling duffle bag was covered with clothes I had packed and unpacked numerous times. I wanted to make sure I was taking my best outfits.

I didn't realize how much I could get done in just a few hours. While Kyra slept, I finished packing all my clothes and made a list of the few things that I still needed to get and things I needed to do before I left town. Victor promised to come by the house and check on things while I was gone for the two weeks. I needed the vacation more than I imagined.

While Kyra slept, I also had time to think. I was accepting way too much from her in the name of love. Finally, when she hit the wall, I realized there was a volatile side of her that I had never before seen. If she was willing to fight with a woman who was staying with her no matter what, how would I know she wouldn't one day take that aggression out on me? I knew I needed to end things, but my heart wasn't ready to say goodbye yet.

"You going somewhere?" Kyra's voice startled me as I obsessed over my travel wardrobe some more.

"Dubai, remember?" I sat back on the couch.

Kyra walked in and sat down on my chaise. "Oh, that's right. I forgot. Damn, when do you leave again?"

"Four days." I smiled.

"Damn, I guess I need to spend as much time with you now as I can." Kyra motioned for me to join her on the chaise.

I walked over and sat next to her. She put her hand on my knee. She was in a much better mood for sure.

"So, ready to talk?" I asked.

"Not really, but I guess we need to," she replied and then firmly pressed her lips tight. "So, the situation is that me and Lisa got into an altercation. When she gets mad, she likes to put her hands on me. And I can only take so much."

Lisa. This was the first time I heard her real name. I never wanted to know her name. Not knowing made her almost not seem real, even though I had met her before.

"Yeah, but why not just leave? You've done this before. How much is enough before you realize maybe you shouldn't be there?"

Kyra lowered her head. "You are absolutely right. That's why the fight started. I went there to get my things. I decided I know where I want to be, and it's with you."

I felt my heart explode. I struggled to remain calm. She got into a fight letting her ex know she was leaving her for me. I had dreamed of the moment that she realized I was the one, but I didn't expect it to happen so soon. But I shouldn't have been so surprised after she told me she loved me.

"I-I don't know what to say."

"Don't say anything. We have some things to figure out. But you're leaving town, and I need to find a new place to stay. So, we'll figure things out when you get back. But until you leave, can I crash here till I find a new place?"

"You don't have your apartment anymore?" I questioned, remembering our first encounter.

Kyra shook her head. "Naw, I was getting rid of it when you came over. That's one of the reasons there was no furniture."

I frowned. I realized she was getting rid of it because she was moving in with Lisa. Loyal had been right all along about her living arrangements.

"So, how about this? I was going to have my friend come by to check on my house. But why don't you just stay here while I'm in Dubai?" I smiled.

"Wait, are you sure? I mean, of course, I'll take care of your crib. But are you sure you're all right with that?"

I nodded. "Yeah, it actually will help me out. I'll feel more comfortable knowing someone is staying here."

Kyra leaned in, planting a sensual kiss on my lips. I felt my heart beating at a rapid pace. She was mine, all mine. I wanted the moment to last forever. Then Kyra stood up.

"I love you, girl. But look, I gotta get ready and get out of here. I gotta go meet up with Howard, and I have a gig tonight. Do you have an extra key, so I don't have to wake you up when I get back tonight?" Kyra walked over and picked up my Beats by Dre headphones. "Do you mind if I borrow these tonight?"

"No, go ahead. And just call me. I can get another key in the morning."

Kyra walked over and kissed me again. "You are something special. You know that, right?"

"I love you too."

Kyra winked at me before heading back to the bedroom. I couldn't help but be giddy. Kyra was mine, and nothing else mattered besides that.

Chapter 23

"Aye, I want something nice back from Dubai. Like a wife or something." Loyal stood at my desk with his sly smile on his face.

"I will see what I can do." I turned off my computer, grabbed the sign I created, and pinned it to the wall, saying, "*Gone to Dubai. Do not contact me.*"

Loyal laughed. "You so damn extra."

I shrugged my shoulders. "That goes for you as well." I stood up and collected my things. I was officially off work and couldn't leave that job quickly enough.

Loyal walked with me toward the front of the call center. I couldn't help but notice the looks as we walked, looks Loyal seemed to be used to. He strolled through the call center with me without a care in the world.

"I'm happy for you. Dubai is on my list. And I think the vacation will do you well."

I patted Loyal on his shoulder. "Okay, I'll bring you back something."

We walked out of the call center and to our cars.

"So, tell me something," Loyal said as he put on his designer sunglasses. "How are things going with Kyra? And don't lie and say you aren't with her."

My face dropped.

"How did you know?"

"I didn't. You just told me." He smirked.

"She left the girl and is looking for a new place to stay. She said she wants to be with me," I boasted.

Loyal wasn't impressed.

"Paige, where is she staying while she looks for a place?" His smirk faded. I pressed my keyless entry and looked away. I wanted to lie but knew he would see right through it. "Paige!"

"It's only for the next couple of days before I go to Dubai."

"Paige, do *not* let that girl stay in your house while you're gone." Loyal's straight face didn't change. I knew he meant it.

"I'm not, I promise. But I really gotta get going. I need to get home and get back out before the stores close."

Loyal's concerned expression made me feel guilty. I knew it was a lie. I had already decided to let Kyra stay as long as she wanted.

We said our goodbyes, and I headed to my house. I arrived home to hear jazz music blasting through the house and the smell of food in

the kitchen. I walked into the kitchen to find
Kyra cooking chicken. The room was a mess, but I
barely noticed it. I was just happy to see her there.

"'Sup, love?" Kyra said as she planted a kiss on
my lips.

"What are you cooking?"

"Chicken and waffles. You hungry, right?" Kyra
flashed a huge smile.

"I am, but I have to run to Torrid real fast. I forgot to get some pajamas for my trip." I pulled a key
out of my pocket and held it up. Kyra looked at me.
"I got this made so you could have one."

Kyra's face brightened. "I really appreciate you
letting me crash here while you're gone. One of
these days, I will pay you back for all the kindness
you've constantly showed me."

"You can start by giving me one of those ten-
ders. They smell amazing." I picked up a piece of
chicken.

"Girl, you can have whatever you like." Kyra sang
like the T.I. song. "Now, get out of here and get
back so we can eat before I head out to my gig tonight."

I left the house floating on cloud nine. Kyra and
I were finally in a relationship, and I loved having
her in my home. I turned on my "love songs" playlist as I drove down the expressway. Finally, things
were looking good for me. I was happy with Kyra

and headed on a luxury vacation I'd been dreaming of taking for years.

Suddenly, an old white pickup truck came out of nowhere, pulling into my lane to get off the exit he was missing. I hit my brakes and swerved, attempting to miss him. Instead, I spun out of control until a huge blow hit my driver's side, and everything went dark.

Chapter 24

I woke up with a pounding headache. The lights were blinding as I attempted to regain my senses. When my eyes finally focused, the first thing I saw was my right foot, wrapped in what seemed to be a bunch of white bandages.

"There she is."

I turned to my right to see my friend Quinn walking toward me with a drink in her hand. "It's about time you woke up." I was shocked to see her. Quinn was stunning. She was dark chocolate and thick in all the right places. She had found a tiny bit of fame when she started posting clothing and wig try-on hauls on YouTube. Now she was a bona fide social media influencer who traveled all over.

"I had an accident." My voice cracked. My throat was parched. I reached for her drink and took a sip. The soda burned going down but provided a little relief.

"You did. Do you not remember what happened?"

I closed my eyes. The whole thing came back to me.

I hit the median when the truck cut me off. The airbags deployed, hitting me in the face and knocking me out for a few moments. When I finally came to, I reached for my phone, but it had fallen on the floor. I wiggled my body just enough to grab it, but the screen was black and cracked. I could hear my text message alerts going off, but I wasn't able to answer or make any calls.

I started to panic when I noticed smoke. What if the car exploded? I tried to open my door, but it wouldn't budge. I was stuck. I looked around, hoping someone would stop. The truck that cut me off wasn't anywhere to be found. He had caused my accident and kept going.

I knew I needed to think. I tried rolling down my window, but it didn't budge. I hit the passenger-side window, and to my luck, it rolled all the way down. I knew I needed to get someone's attention. I watched as cars sped past, but no one stopped to aid me. I was on the expressway, so surely, someone saw what happened but wasn't concerned enough to stop. Finally, I noticed a police car in my rearview. I tried to wave my hand, but he passed me without noticing. I started to panic.

"Help!" I yelled over and over. "Why won't anyone help me?" I cried. Suddenly, I noticed a clothing bag I hadn't taken out of my car the day before. I grabbed it, throwing the shirt I had

bought on the passenger seat. I took the bag and began waving it feverishly out the passenger-side door. Hopefully, someone would come to my aid.

After a few minutes, a beat-up pickup truck slowed down. Then they pulled in front of me. An older gentleman and his child hopped out of the car and rushed to the passenger side.

"Don't worry, ma'am. We saw what happened. We got off and turned around to help. My son is calling 911. Can you move?"

"I-I can't feel my foot," I cried.

The man held his hands up. "Don't try to move at all. Help will be here soon."

It only took a few moments for an ambulance and two police cars to arrive. The fireman came up to the passenger-side window. He asked if I could open my door. A stupid question, I thought as my door was smashed into the median.

"Don't try to move. We'll probably have to cut you out," he explained. Of course, I wasn't trying to hear it.

"I'm okay. Just open the passenger door." I unhooked my seat belt.

"Ma'am, I think you should just relax."

"No." I started pulling myself to the passenger's side. My foot was numb but wasn't hurting, so I felt that was a good sign.

Two firefighters joined in as the EMTs pulled the stretcher up to the door. They pulled me out the rest of the way and placed me on the stretcher.

I couldn't completely focus. So many things were running through my head. First, I had to be okay. I was leaving for Dubai in a few days.

In the ambulance, I begged the EMT to call someone. I couldn't think of any numbers except my best friend, Mina. So I gave them her number.

"I can't be hurt. I'm going to Dubai in three days. I have to go to Dubai."

"Don't worry about that right now," the younger white EMT assured me. "You will make it to Dubai; just relax."

"I will?" I gave a big sigh of relief.

"Ma'am," the older Black EMT looked at me and pointed at my foot, "look at your foot." I looked down to see my foot leaning to the left. "You're not getting on anyone's plane anytime soon. Now, please, try to calm down. We're going to take good care of you."

I sat there looking at my mangled foot. Tears fell from my eyes. "My best friend is gonna kill me."

I snapped back to reality. I looked at Quinn. She tried to smile, although I could see the concern in her eyes.

"How did you know to come here?"

"Well," my friend Quinn sat in the chair next to my bed, "you had the EMTs call Mina. She called Morgan because, of course, there wasn't anything she could do being out of town. Morgan was at work and called me. I just got back to town, so was able to come straight here. Seems you were entertaining the guy in the bed next to you earlier. When I got here, he asked if I was looking for the girl named Dubai."

I turned my head. The bed was empty. "Where is he now?"

"I'm guessing jail." Quinn shrugged. "He was handcuffed to his bed when I got here."

Two nurses came over to my bed. One pudgy white nurse checked my fluids while the petite woman scribbled something on a board.

"All right, we are about to move you to your room."

"I need to make a phone call."

"You can do that when you get to your room," one of the nurses said as he unlocked the wheels on my bed.

Quinn followed the aides as they moved me to a regular room. I had so much on my mind. Morgan and Tara arrived just as I made it to my room. Tara told me she had already let my job know so I could get my short-term disability paperwork in. I attempted to listen as my friends talked about my situation and how they felt when they got the phone calls alerting them of my accident. In addition, they informed my family, who was also headed over to me. I was thankful, but there was one person who I knew I needed to speak to.

"Morgan," I said. Morgan walked up to my bed. "I need you to call Kyra. Tell her what happened."

Morgan looked confused by the request, but she could tell from my expression that I didn't want to explain. She pulled her phone out and dialed Kyra's number. I listened as she informed Kyra of what had happened.

"She said she's on the way," Morgan whispered. I could tell she wasn't happy, but she also didn't want to say anything to cause me extra stress.

Visiting hours were ending. I finally convinced my friends and family to go home. I sat in the modest hospital room with my thoughts. My ankle was so severely dislocated that I wasn't going to be able to put weight on it for at least a month. And due to my size, I would be bedridden for the near future. I was numb as I listened as doctors and hospital administrators explained the situation to my aunt and friends. I would be moved to their local nursing and rehabilitation center in the morning, where I would spend the next month. Mina arranged to postpone our trip, but I couldn't help but feel like I had ruined everything.

The day was almost over, and it already felt like I had been there for weeks. On top of that, I didn't know what was taking Kyra so long to get to the hospital. With visiting hours ending, I didn't know if I would see her at all. Now, I was alone, staring at the little flat screen attached to the white wall.

A Different World was playing on TVOne, but the sound was muted. I couldn't even enjoy one of my favorite episodes.

Suddenly, I heard a faint knock on my door. I turned my head as the door cracked open.

"Thank you, baby." I heard the familiar accent echo through the door. My heart skipped a beat as Kyra walked into my room with a sullen smile on her face. "Hey, you." She walked up to my bed and put her hand on my thigh.

"You came." I smiled.

"Of course." Kyra pulled the reclining chair close to the bed. "I'm not supposed to be here, but the nurse let me come in. How you feeling?"

The moments from the day flooded my mind. I couldn't speak. Tears welled in my eyes. I finally had what I wanted. Kyra was not only living with me but was mine, and I wasn't going to be home to enjoy it.

"I'm sorry." I wept.

Kyra wiped the tears from my eyes. "Boo, don't trip. I got you. I'll keep the house together and come over here every chance I get. If you need anything, I'll bring it. We will get through this together."

Kyra rested her palm on my cheek. Her warm hand soothed my aching soul. I was in a difficult situation with a long haul in front of me. But with Kyra by my side, I knew things would work out.

Chapter 25

"Come on, Paige, you can do better than that."

A month had come and gone. Finally, I received the bad news that I would be stuck in the rehab facility for another month. With my weight and the severity of my injury, I was still unable to walk. My life had become an endless round of nurses waking me up constantly for random things. I was miserable and couldn't see the light at the end of the tunnel. The one saving grace was the friendship I formed with my physical therapist, Mario. Mario was my age and came into my room cracking jokes from our first encounter.

My friends still came by to check on me, but their visits had become less frequent. Now, I mostly see people on weekends, leaving me alone with my thoughts during the week. I had my computer, so I wrote as much as possible, but I lacked motivation on most days. I was slipping into a depression being stuck in the small room.

"I'm trying," I said as I stretched my leg back and forth. Mario instantly knew I was lying by the expression on his face. He was right. I wasn't feeling it at all. "I don't want to do this today."

Mario sat on the stool next to me. "What's going on, Paige? You all right?"

"I don't want to be here anymore, Mario. I'm losing my mind."

There was more to it, and I knew it. I hadn't seen Kyra in almost two weeks. Her last visit was simply to drop off my computer and a few things from my house, and even then, she didn't stay but a few moments. Now, whenever I call, she doesn't answer. And she would only call me back late at night—and sometimes, not at all. Her texts were few and far between. She claimed she was busy with the bands and gigs, but I couldn't shake the feeling that there was more than that.

Mario stood up. "I know what you need." He took the weights off my legs and unlocked the wheels on my wheelchair. "Let's roll."

I didn't know where we were going, but I didn't care. Mario pushed me swiftly down the hallway and to the elevator door. We made it down to the main floor, a floor I hadn't seen since I moved to the seventh-floor rehabilitation level. The wind against my face was refreshing as Mario guided me through the long corridors of the hospital floor. Finally, he stopped at two large blue doors, pressed his badge against the keycard, and waited on the doors to open.

My eyes widened as we entered a beautiful atrium filled with lush green plants and flowers. A few benches and chairs were spread out around a large koi pond in the middle with a fountain cascading down it. In the corner stood a statue of some biblical figure I didn't recognize. Mario pulled me up to a table and sat next to me.

"Wow, I didn't know this was here," I said as I looked around, soaking in the atmosphere.

"That's because you're not supposed to know about it. This is like a Zen spot for hospital workers. We can bring patients here if we want to, but we mostly keep it to ourselves. I love coming here. Relaxing, isn't it?"

I looked at Mario and never realized how attractive he was until that moment. His broad shoulders protruded through his tight-fitting scrubs. He also had locs that hung down to his shoulders. He pulled them back into a nice, braided style, so they weren't in his face. His teeth were perfectly straight and white, and he always smelled great. He was shorter than most men I found attractive, but that didn't matter.

"So, what's wrong with you, Paige?"

I thought about Kyra. "Nothing. I'll be all right."

Mario shook his head. "Come on now. I'd hope you know by now you can trust me. We are homies."

I needed a release. I didn't like talking to my friends about Kyra. I had finally come clean about

Kyra and me reconnecting and her living in my house. This infuriated them. They offered to do everything from random pop-ups at my home to evict her. Whenever they asked about her, I would lie. I'd tell them that she had just left the hospital or was on her way later after practice. I wanted to keep the facade going, even if it was only in my mind.

"It's my girlfriend, or whatever she is."

"Chick with the poofy hair? The musician?" Mario didn't take his eyes off me.

"Yes, she hasn't been around much. She's living in my house, and I barely hear from her. I don't know what to think anymore."

"Why don't you have someone go by and check on your crib?" he asked with a straight expression.

I sat for a moment. It was an easy option. Multiple people had keys to my house. If I made one phone call to them, they would show up and take care of Kyra in a heartbeat. The thought was intriguing. I did wonder what she was up to. I had been lying so much to my friends and myself lately that I couldn't do it anymore.

"Honestly, I'm afraid." I lowered my head.

"Afraid of what?"

"Of what they might learn when they go there. I don't think I could handle anything besides what I'm already dealing with."

The fountain's falling water hitting the pond echoed through the atrium as we sat in silence. Mario put his hand on my shoulder. It felt good having it there.

"Paige, when I met you, I knew there was something special about you. You have a light in you that not many have. Even in this shitty situation, you have been making the best of it. Working on the rehab and the nursing home floors, I see tons of people just be there—no friends, no family. It can be very humbling and depressing at times. But you have a whole tribe behind you. Do you know how many Edible Arrangements you've gotten? Seriously, you gotta be tired of eating pineapples and strawberries." Mario laughed. I couldn't help but chuckle a bit too.

"So, you're why my Edible Arrangements always seem like they're missing fruit," I smirked.

"Listen, a man's gotta eat." Mario's laugh was infectious. He giggled for a minute before his serious expression returned. "But seriously, you have so many who love you, so why are you focusing so much energy on someone who doesn't seem like they deserve to be in your life?"

I sat with the question. I didn't know the answer to it. Kyra had consumed so much of my life for the last year, and I couldn't understand why. Did she ever deserve my love? I knew the answer was no, but for some reason, my heart just didn't want to believe it yet.

I dreaded the trek back to my room. I was emotionally drained and didn't want to be alone in my room. Mario opened my room door to find a huge Edible Arrangement and two new floral arrangements sitting on the ledge of my window.

As he walked over to get the cards from them, he said, "See, girl, you got people in your corner. Focus on them and yourself. Oh, and I'm eating some more of that fruit."

Mario helped me back into my bed. Once comfortable, I opened the cards attached to the arrangements. The flowers were sent from a friend in New York, while the other arrangement and fruit came from two fans of my books. A warm sensation filled my body. I did have people who cared about me enough to send me gifts to brighten my day, and here I was focusing my energy on someone who wasn't concerned enough about me even to text me back. I was over it and over Kyra. It was time I ended things with her once and for all.

"Hey, you."

Mario and I both turned our heads to see Kyra standing at the door. She looked disheveled like she hadn't slept in days. Mario stood next to my bed, unmoved by her presence.

"Kyra, what are you doing here?" I said as I raised the back of my bed.

"I was in the area, so I thought I would check on ya." She looked at Mario and then back at me. Kyra walked up and held out her hand. "My bad. I don't think we have met."

Mario reluctantly shook her hand. "I'm Mario, Paige's therapist. And you are?"

"Kyra, her woman." Kyra and Mario stared at each other. You could slice the tension with a knife.

"Oh, you're Kyra. I have heard so much about you. But honestly, since I haven't seen you around, I thought you were only a character she was making up for a new book." Mario smirked as Kyra's dimples faded. I wanted to laugh but couldn't. "Well, I'll leave you guys. Paige, see you later."

Mario walked out of the room but not before giving Kyra one more disapproving gaze. He closed the door behind him, and she sat down.

"Physical therapist, huh? Seems like he might want to do more than just work you out." Kyra plopped down in the recliner.

I was instantly annoyed by her presence, which had never happened before. She looked dusty and broke down, and I didn't want her in my room.

"Kyra, what's up?" I completely ignored her statements about Mario. The idea of her being jealous was humorous.

"Damn, did I interrupt something? You been blowing up my phone and shit, and I take time out of my day to come over here to see you, and this is how you act?" Kyra's voice deepened.

"I've been blowing up your phone? I've been trying to check on you and my house when I shouldn't have to call you at all. I haven't seen you in weeks. Barely heard from you, and you come here with an attitude."

Kyra jumped up. "Look, I've been out here busting my ass, playing gig after gig so I can make money to contribute to the house. I'm sorry I haven't been by here, but a nigga been working."

I wasn't in the mood for any of it. I didn't care about her reasons anymore. I was over it all. She had pissed me off one too many times. Kyra took a deep breath as she walked up to my bed and put her hand on my shoulder.

"Paige, I'm sorry. I know I've fucked up. I'm really out here trying to do everything I can to be a good woman for you. I don't want you coming home and having to take care of everything. I want to be able to help you out. I didn't even realize it had been weeks since I've been working so hard. So please don't be mad, baby."

Kyra rubbed her hands against my cheek. She leaned in, planting a deep kiss on my lips. I felt my wall breaking down with each caress on my face.

"I miss you, boo," Kyra whispered as her lips slowly made their way down my cheek to my neck. She nibbled on my earlobe before the tip of her tongue danced down my neck. Then she placed her hand on my swollen nipple that was peeking up under my nightgown. "Tell me you missed me too."

My mind wanted to say I didn't, but my body rebelled. My vagina began to throb. After being poked and prodded for over a month, my body craved her intimate touch.

"Tell me you missed me," Kyra repeated as her hands made their way under my nightgown. She pinched my nipple, causing a tidal wave of heat to flood from between my legs.

"I missed you," I gasped, wanting more—needing more.

Kyra walked over to the hospital room door. She locked it and quickly came back. Within moments, her hand disappeared into my underwear. Her index finger moved in circles on my clit for a few moments before slipping inside my wetness.

"Kyra," I moaned as she finger fucked me into a frenzy. I grabbed the guard rail on my bed, closing my eyes as she continued. Finally, her lips touched my lips again. I didn't want her kisses; I *needed* them more than anything else in the world at that moment.

"You tell that therapist that this . . ." Kyra pushed her fingers deeper inside of me, causing me to let out a moan, "belongs to me. Stick to his day job before I have to fuck up that nigga." With that, she pushed them as deep as she could.

I grabbed her shoulder as my body orgasmed, causing my essence to cover her hand. She smiled as she pulled her hand out of my panties and placed her two wet fingers inside her mouth.

"I need you to get home soon so I can enjoy *that* again," she said as she walked over to wash the rest of me off her hands. My heart was racing as I tried to catch my breath.

Finally, Kyra unlocked the door, then walked over, sitting back in the recliner chair. Her phone began to ring. She pressed ignore and went to type a message.

"Yeah, so I gotta run, practice for this gig tomorrow. Hey, about the cable bill? Do you want to give me the money to pay for it or what? I noticed the internet was out, and I turned the TV on, and a message came on that said it wasn't on."

"I turned it off," I replied. "I mean, you said you're never really there, and I'm not, so I figured why should I be paying a bill for something that's not being used?"

Kyra frowned. "Well, actually, I was using the internet. I was doing some research on some stuff I'm trying to write. But I guess I understand. Guess I'll have to go *all* the way to the library *if* I can make it in time."

"You want me to turn it back on, don't you?" I started to lower down my bed.

"It would be nice if you could. It would make things much easier on me. Oh, and if you don't mind, could you PayPal me $100? I want to go ahead and take care of a few things around the house that need fixing. For example, you need some new lightbulbs and could use a new shower-head in the guest bathroom."

"Yeah, I never use that bathroom, so I totally forgot about that. But wait, you've been using one of the guest bedrooms?"

"No, I just took a shower there to see if it was the same as your room. It definitely isn't."

As Kyra stood up to leave, I nodded my head. I picked up my phone, sent her the money on PayPal, and opened my Comcast account to pay the bill. Kyra kissed me and promised to return before the end of the weekend. I smiled, happy, knowing that she was still mine. All my reservations about her flew out of the window. Not only did she still care, but I knew she would do better, especially with her thinking there was someone else up here who wanted me. Although Mario was not a threat, I would keep him in my back pocket to keep her in line. As long as she thought someone else wanted me, she would act right. At least, I hoped she would.

Chapter 26

I sat in the small examination room waiting on my orthopedic surgeon to arrive. I was drained and completely over the entire experience. It was going on my third month of living in the rehabilitation facility. What I thought would be a month at the most turned into almost three months of being bedridden and unable to put any weight on my foot. I no longer looked forward to these visits. Every time I hoped for some good news, I was hit with, "We need more time, Paige." I missed my life, my home, and I missed Kyra.

Three more weeks passed with no word from her since the last visit. Finally, she told me she was going back to New Orleans to do some gigs and visit with her family for a few weeks. The infrequent texts were back, and phone calls had disappeared completely. I had reached the breaking point where I just didn't care about her or anything else. I only wanted to be able to walk again.

The door to the room opened, and my surgeon walked in with the hospital administrator. I perked up. I had never seen the admin in the visits. I hoped it meant good news. Instead, I quickly noticed the expression on her face. My heart sank. I knew it was going to be more bad news.

My surgeon, Dr. Sullivan, was an older Black man who I knew was liked by many of the staff in the facility. He was upbeat and personable, unlike the other surgeons who came to check on their patients. His salt-and-pepper hair always looked like he had just left the barbershop, and he always smelled fantastic. He rolled his stool close to me.

"All right, Paige, we have some news for you. Good and, well, honestly, bad." Dr. Sullivan raised my foot. "Good news is this is coming off today."

"Oh my God!" I screamed with joy. My blue cast was covered in doodles from my friends, but I was ready for it to go. I turned my head to see Mrs. Love, the administrator leaning against the wall. "Wait, what's the bad news?"

Mrs. Love took a deep breath and opened the manila folder she was holding. I knew she couldn't be older than Dr. Sullivan, but she looked much older. I chalked it up to his excellent melanin. Her hands were very wrinkled, like her face with many crow's feet around her eyes.

"Paige, we have a bit of a problem. It seems your job, well, they canceled your insurance."

"Wait, what?" I looked at her. There wasn't a smile in the room. "That can't be right."

"I talked to them all morning. It seems as though you haven't made a payment on your insurance since being in here, so they not only canceled, but they backdated it to the day you arrived."

I felt like someone knocked the wind out of me.

"I don't understand. They take my insurance out with my disability they give me weekly. I need to call them."

"Yes, you can check, but they seem to be stating there is nothing that can be done. This also means we must discharge you."

"Excuse me?"

Dr. Sullivan put his hand on my knee. "The good thing is that you can start putting weight on your foot again. The bad thing is that you still need physical therapy and will have to pay for that out of pocket."

"And don't worry, we will send you home with everything we can on us. But you need to call your family and inform them you are leaving tomorrow. And we will work with you on the bill."

They continued to try to reassure me that things would work out, but I couldn't concentrate on anything they were saying.

"What's the bill?" I questioned. I had been in the facility for almost three months and knew that I probably couldn't afford it.

Mrs. Love handed me the envelope. I opened it to see close to $80,000 written in red. I couldn't breathe. The room started spinning. I could hear her telling me to calm down, but all I could do was cry hysterically.

"Paige, don't worry. Things *will* work out. We will work with you as much as possible," she reassured me. I wanted to punch her in her face. How could she stand in front of me and tell me things were going to be all right while handing me a bill I couldn't afford?

Dr. Sullivan put his hand on my knee. "Paige, I know this is a lot to take in. But right now, we need to focus on the positive. You are getting out of this cast today. And we will get you as prepared to go home as we possibly can."

"Dr. Sullivan is right. We will have our van take you home at no charge. And they will make sure you are comfortable before leaving."

I couldn't speak. I just stared at them. Mrs. Love knew there was nothing else she could say. She exited the room, leaving me with Dr. Sullivan. His professional demeanor loosened the moment the door closed.

"Paige, look, I know this is some bullshit. So I'm going to help you out. I'm making sure you have your boot and plenty of meds to take home. And listen, I'm going to send a bag to your room, so make sure your people grab it and take as much shit as you can from your room that you might need."

I looked at Dr. Sullivan's serious expression. He was looking out for me. This softened the blow just a little.

"Thank you," I muttered. It was all I could say.

I was silent while the assistant came in to remove my cast and get me bandaged with my new boot. I tried to listen to what they told me, but I couldn't focus. I wanted to get back to my room and figure out how this was happening.

Finally, I was rolled back to my room. I grabbed my cell phone and texted Kyra to let her know what was happening. I then called my human resources department. After being transferred multiple times, I was informed that due to changes, they no longer took insurance out of disability payments. Because I now owed around $200 to my company insurance plan, they had decided to cancel and backdate the cancellation. I argued that I still worked at the job and should be allowed to pay the amount, but they didn't care about my dilemma in a typical corporate fashion. I knew there was nothing I was going to accomplish from the hospital bed. I had less than twenty-four hours to get all my affairs together. I was headed home, a moment I had dreamed about since the day of my accident, but due to the situation, it was bittersweet.

News of my situation spread like wildfire. Multiple staff members tending to me during this time came to wish me well and express their displeasure with my company. I knew they were only trying to help, but I didn't want to speak to anyone anymore. I just wanted to get things over with. I called my aunts and friends to let them know what was happening. My family members jumped into action, stating they would be there to get me settled and take care of anything I needed. Kyra still hadn't responded to my text message. So I sent another one telling her I needed to speak to her ASAP. I didn't want to inform her I was coming home through text. I wanted to see if she would contact me.

Mario walked into my room holding a bag. He closed the door behind him and walked over to my bed. His usual smile had faded. I knew he was aware of the situation too.

"I know you got a lot on your mind, so I just wanted to drop this off." He placed the bag on top of my duffle bag. "It's got ACE bandages and some other stuff in it I swiped from the therapy room. These should get you through the next month, for sure. And I'm more than willing to help you at your house if you need me to. Shit is fucked up, man. I hate our healthcare system so much."

"Thank you, Mario. You have been a bright light for me during this dark moment." I forced a smile.

He placed his hand on my arm. "I know, I'm awesome."

My phone rang. I looked at the number. It seemed familiar, but I couldn't place where. I pressed the speaker button and said, "Hello."

"You've received a collect phone call from—" Kyra's voice appeared on the phone—"an inmate in Shelby County Jail."

Mario and I looked at each other. I was embarrassed and angry. What could she have done to end up back in jail again? Nevertheless, I accepted the phone call.

"Give me a moment," I said as I took the call off speaker.

"Do your thing. I'll check back on you later." Mario was worried but left my room anyway.

"Kyra."

"Hey, babe. Sorry to call you like this."

"What happened now?"

"I will explain when I get out. Can you call Howard for me please to get me out?"

I wanted to say no. I held the phone for a moment contemplating the situation. But this was too much on me. I had my own issues to deal with, and bailing her out was just another expense I didn't need.

"Kyra, this is some bullshit. I am getting released tomorrow, and I gotta worry about your ass instead of my own issues."

"You getting released? Um, okay. Well, I need to get out to be at the house when you get there."

Kyra's voice shifted a bit. She actually sounded concerned.

I knew she was right. She had my key and had been in my house this entire time. I knew my friends and family would help me, but the person who should be there for me was locked up. If I didn't get her out, I knew it meant the end of us. I knew she would never forgive me. But I wanted answers, and I knew Kyra wouldn't give them to me. The one-minute warning chimed on the phone.

"I'll call him now."

We hung up, and I called Howard.

"Ms. Paige, I've already heard from Kyra. She told me you would be calling to pay the bail." Howard's voice rang through my speaker.

"Mr. Howard, what did she do this time?"

He sighed. "Paige, I don't know you personally. I've known Kyra for a long time, and I know this isn't my place, but you need to let this be the last time you help her. She will constantly get into fights with women."

I was furious. While ignoring my calls, she fought with her ex again. I wanted to hang up and leave her rotting in jail, but I knew I needed her at the house.

"I can't believe she got into another fight with that woman."

"No," Howard paused for a second. "Honestly, I was surprised when she told me you would be calling. It happened at your house, so I thought it was with you. But it wasn't with Lisa."

My heart dropped. Kyra had another woman in *my* house and had gotten into a physical altercation with her. I felt the room spinning.

"I've been in the hospital for a while. Kyra was staying at my place." I couldn't believe it. I wanted it to be a lie, but I knew it wasn't.

We sat silently on the phone for a moment before Howard chimed back in.

"Paige, I hope you feel better. And please, get her out of your house."

I finished giving my information to Howard and hung up. My mind was racing. There was another woman in my home, a new woman I knew nothing about.

A nurse walked in, and I quickly asked her to leave. I needed to be alone. I didn't want to be bothered for the rest of the night. I just wanted to get home and get rid of Kyra for good.

Chapter 27

The drive was unnerving. I was going home, finally, after three months of hospital beds, lousy food, killer therapy sessions, and nursing assistants who sucked at their jobs. I wanted to be happy, but the feeling was bittersweet. Thank goodness the staff was nice enough to provide me with a plethora of pills and my newly purchased boot for my messed-up foot. My aunt grabbed the walker and wheelchair we had from when my grandmother used it before she passed. Then she and my mother followed the hospital van to my house.

I wanted to be excited. I was going home. I would finally be back in my fortress of solitude, with my large HD TV and all my channels. Not to mention my PlayStation, Xbox, and everything else I didn't have in the hospital to occupy my time. I knew I had to deal with the Kyra situation, but for the moment, I just wanted to be happy to finally be out of the hospital, no matter how fucked-up the situation might have been.

I wanted to focus on the positive, but the Kyra situation only infuriated me. There had been *another* woman in my house, probably also in *my* bed. Finally, I had to realize that Kyra was never going to be who I thought she could be and was. It hurt, but I knew it was time to face the ugly truth.

I watched out the window as familiar places passed by. We were getting closer, and an awful feeling crept into my stomach. I was nervous about being on my own without professional help. I thought about making Kyra stay just to assist me. After all, she owed me at least that. But I knew in the end she wouldn't be helpful. Many more late nights and ignored phone calls would take place. If I had to heal, I was better off doing it alone.

Things could have been a lot worse. At least I was finally able to put weight on my foot. And Mario and my friend Kimberly, who was also a physical therapist, offered to come to the house and help me with therapy since I no longer had insurance. I was going to be okay, but I had some major hurdles to overcome. Mario had stayed with me after his shift ended to help me get used to walking wearing my boot. It was painful, but with the walker, it was tolerable. The first hurdle would be the steps to my front door. I made a mental note to start looking into making my house ADA accessible. I didn't realize how unprepared my house was.

The moment had arrived. The driver pulled into my driveway. The uneasy feeling was turning into full panic by now. I was not ready. How was I going to make this happen? I wanted to return to the facility I had dreamed about leaving every day for three months.

Then I noticed a familiar face walking toward me. Kevin, one of Kyra's bandmates, was headed toward my van. I didn't know why he was there, but I welcomed his strong arms. He could assist me with the two steps I was worried about.

"Hey, um, I didn't know you were coming back today," Kevin said.

"Yeah, it was an unexpected thing," I replied as the van driver unhooked the latches keeping me in place in the van. I handed my keys to my aunt, and she headed to the house with my mother.

Kevin frowned. "Oh, um, Kyra isn't here. I was coming to scoop her, but I don't know where she is." There was something strange about his look. It wasn't a concern; it was worry. I realized not only had Kyra not gotten out of jail yet, but Kevin was oblivious to what was happening.

"She had to take care of some things, but she'll be back today." I forced a happy face.

Just then, I saw my aunt's silver hair walking toward the van. There was no smile. She looked angry. She said hello to Kevin before turning her face toward me.

"Paige, your house is a mess," she said in a soft, very proper tone.

"What?" I was confused. I looked at Kevin. His expression said it all. He knew *exactly* what she was talking about.

"Ma'am, my name is Kevin. I'm friends with Kyra and can help get the house in order. I don't think she knew that Paige was coming back today." He offered his hand. My aunt, always the proper one, shook it and offered as warm a smile as she could.

"It's bad, Paige. It's horrendous. What on earth were you all doing in there?" My aunt turned back to Kevin.

Kevin put his hands up as if a cop had busted him. "Oh, I don't know. I just know Kyra has been really busy. We were supposed to have practice, and I have no idea where she is."

"Well, let's just get Paige in. Do you mind helping?" As the van driver pushed me in the borrowed wheelchair, my aunt led the way. Kevin followed and was more than willing to assist.

As we moved closer to my front door, I could hear my mother's voice coming from my place. Her tone wasn't as demure as my aunt's. A recovering drug addict who had been on the streets her entire life, her words included profanity, whereas my aunt never cursed.

"Who is this bitch that did this shit to my daughter's house? She better not show her ass up while

I'm here, or I'm fucking her up." My mother's voice rang out from behind the windows.

I was now worried. What was I about to walk into?

"I'm so sorry, Paige." Kevin lowered his head.

My heart was beating fast. I wanted to get into the house and see what the big deal was. Kyra was probably just a little junkie. I remembered when she cooked, she was messy, which I knew would bother my clean freaks aunt and mom.

Kevin and the van driver helped me up out of the wheelchair. I stood still for a moment, attempting to get used to the pain as it shot through my foot. Kevin caught me in his muscular arms. The pain was excruciating. I knew walking up the steps wasn't going to work. I had to figure out another way. The driver and Kevin hovered as they attempted to help me, but I quickly became defeated.

"Oh, fuck it," I said as I slid down the wall. I crawled up the two steps, pulling my bad leg behind me. Kevin and the van driver stood by, on alert just in case I couldn't make it. The hard floor was killing my knees, but not nearly as bad as trying to walk up those steps.

My aunt held the door open as I crawled into the house. My eyes widened in shock. My hallway floor wasn't its regular color. Instead, it was covered in dust and dirt. A smell of old grease hit my nostrils. This couldn't be my house. No way it was.

"Paige, whoever this bitch is that's been here needs her ass kicked." I saw my mother's feet appear as I sat in the doorway on my hands and knees. My mother turned to Kevin, who was attempting to help me off the floor. "And I know that's yo' friend, but I don't give a fuck. Did you help this bitch make this mess?"

"No, ma'am, I didn't have anything to do with this. But I am sorry you are coming home to it. I will stay and personally get all of this cleaned up. I know the other day, Kyra was cooking for an event. I don't think she had time to clean it up—"

"No!" My mother cut Kevin's apologetic voice off. "This shit doesn't happen in a day. You all have treated my daughter's place like a crack house."

I felt my chest tightening. I let go of Kevin and started to crawl on my knees toward my living room. The grainy dirt from the floor stuck to my hands and knees as I crawled through the hallway. It didn't get better. Dirt was everywhere. I had no idea where that much dirt even came from. I maneuvered from one room 'til I made it to my living room. I didn't focus on the floor until making it to my oversized chair. I turned over on my butt and used my arms to push myself into the chair. That was one thing therapy was good for. My upper body strength was a lot better. Kevin ran over and assisted me, making sure I made it on the chair.

"I'm going to get this stuff cleaned up for Kyra.
I'm sure she'll be back later and get things completely together."

Finally settled on my chair, my heart dropped.
The room was filthy. Unfamiliar clothes, papers,
and various instruments covered my couch, purchased only a month before my accident. My coffee
table was so filled I couldn't see the cherry blos-
som tree design that covered the top of it. Then
my eyes shifted to my entertainment system. Now,
my blood went from boiling to inferno seeing my
system completely dismantled. My soundbar and
game systems were pulled out with various cords
hanging from the television and scattered on the
floor.

I couldn't talk. I could barely breathe. The
sound of my aunt and mother bickering zoned
out. I felt the room spinning. I didn't understand.
What—how—why was this happening? I knew I
needed to stay calm. There was nothing I could do.
My day went from bad to fucking tragic in an instant. I didn't think anything else could go wrong.

Suddenly, my aunt and mother stopped bickering. The room was quiet. I couldn't stop staring
at my entertainment system. My eyes started losing focus, but I refused to cry. I couldn't let anyone
in that room see just how upset I was because that
would do nothing but cause more panic.

Then my aunt walked into the living room. She put her hand on my shoulder. I looked up at the concerned expression covering her face.

"Paige, there are prophylactics on the floor in your bedroom." Her voice was calm but concerning.

"Oh, hell no!" My mother's voice blared like a megaphone throughout the house. "Why the fuck is all this perverted sex shit on the fucking floor? Lube, condom wrappers, and some other shit."

Now, I *really* zoned out. I didn't want to hear anything else. I closed my eyes, hoping that if I kept them closed long enough, I would open my eyes, and things would be back to normal. Kevin lowered his head in shame. He knew there was no excuse he could come up with for Kyra on that one. My mother was yelling at the top of her lungs. The hospital driver didn't know if he should stay or go. I couldn't stop staring at my entertainment system. I just wanted everything to stop.

"Where is this bitch? I'm going to *kill* her." My mother stormed into the room. "Where is your friend?"

"Yvonne, calm down. Do you want someone to call the police on you for being so loud?" My aunt, somehow, kept her same calm tone.

"I don't give a fuck if they do. I ain't afraid of jail. I've gone to jail for a lot less." My mother rushed over to Kevin, who jumped back. "Where is your little friend?"

"Mom, chill out!" I yelled. I couldn't take anymore. "Kyra doesn't go in my room. That was left
over from before I had the accident."

I didn't know why I lied. I just wanted all the
noise to stop. Kevin looked at me. He knew I was
covering for her, and from his expression, he
couldn't understand why either. I didn't know
where Kyra was, but I knew this would be the last
time I ever saved her ass.

I listened to my mother chastise me for the condoms. I knew she didn't completely believe the
story but could only go by my word. I didn't understand why Kyra was using condoms either.

The driver brought my things in, then headed
back to the hospital. Kevin helped my aunt and
mother with a few things before leaving. He left his
number and told me to call if I needed anything. I
sat in my recliner, still staring at my entertainment
system while my mother and aunt swept through
my home like a cleaning tornado. My phone was
constantly ringing, but I didn't want to talk to anyone. I just wanted to wake up from this god-awful
dream.

Everyone had thoroughly cleaned my house two
hours later, but it still didn't feel like my home. I
put on a happy face and thanked my aunt and
mother. They brought me some food and ensured I
could walk well enough with the walker. I assured
them I could make it through the night on my own

and that I just needed to be alone for a while. The last thing I wanted was for my mother to stay at my house. They made me show them I could walk to and from my bathroom and get up and down off my toilet before they left.

I finally had my home to myself, and I had never felt so alone and miserable before in my life.

Chapter 28

I sat in the darkness. I didn't want to turn on any lights or the television. I just wanted to wallow in my misery. I didn't know what I did to deserve such awful Karma, but I just wanted to beg for it to end. I didn't know how much more I could take.

Kyra still hadn't returned to my home and wasn't responding to text messages. I finally had broken down and sent her a scathing thread of messages. I went off about everything. How she had a woman in my house and how I wanted all my money back from bailing her out. My texts went from angry to hurt to confusion. She wasn't even woman enough to face me. Kevin had texted to check on me multiple times, but the woman who caused all my anguish was nowhere to be found.

I wanted answers, but I knew that I still wouldn't get the answers I deserved whenever she did show up. I looked over at the pile of her junk on my couch. I noticed a black tip under the edge of the sofa. It was my computer I had allowed her to use.

I hobbled over and used the end of the walker to push the computer back toward my recliner. I picked it up and opened it. She had the nerve to set up her own login and password on my laptop. I smiled. Password or not, I was the administrator. I logged in to my profile and unlocked her profile.

The second her screen pulled up, I was hit with the truth. Her Facebook was open, and two open messages from two different women were visible. I read them. One, a Taylor James, was the one with whom she had gotten into the fight. There was a long message telling Kyra never to contact her again and that that would be the last time she ever put her hands on her. They had been dealing with each other for a long time. I read the responses from Kyra. She wasn't apologizing for what she did. Instead, she told the girl that she wasn't going anywhere and that Taylor knew that in the end, she loved her. The words cut me like a knife to my chest. She was telling another woman she loved her while living off me.

I clicked on Taylor's profile picture. She had blocked Kyra. I grabbed my phone and opened my Facebook app, typed in her name, and she popped right up. Her profile was mainly private. I could see she was beautiful and a realtor. I noticed we had one mutual friend in common, my friend Missy. I immediately called Missy.

"Hey, Miss Lady, I heard you got out of the hospital. I was going to call you in the morning." Missy's usual peppy voice echoed through my speaker.

"Hey, girl, yeah, I got out today." I had no interest in small talk. I was on a mission. "So, this might sound crazy, but I noticed we have a mutual friend. Do you know Taylor James?"

"Taylor? Yes, that's my girl. She sold me my house. Why?"

I thought for a minute about what I wanted to divulge to Missy. I considered her a friend but wasn't sure I thought of her as that much of a friend. But desperate times called for desperate measures, and I wanted answers.

"This might seem crazy, but I think she got into a fight in my house with a girl named Kyra staying here."

"Kyra? The musician Kyra? I mean, yeah, they used to date. Remember, I mentioned Kyra at your book release, and I wondered why she was there. But I don't think Taylor would be at your house. Taylor has a huge house in Collierville. She's a realtor in the Million-Dollar Club. And they stopped messing around a long time ago." Missy sounded genuinely concerned and confused.

I took a deep breath. I couldn't hold it in. The words came up like word vomit. I told Missy all about Kyra, the arrest, and how I found my house when I got home. I explained that I just wanted answers, to know what happened in my house and that her friend might be my only way to find out.

"Oh my God, Paige, I am in shock. I'm going to call her right now. Do you mind if I give her your number?"

"No, feel free."

We hung up, and I felt a little better. But then worry set in. I wondered what was going to happen next. Would Taylor call me? Would she try to get mad that her business was now spread to her friend? My phone rang several minutes after I ended the call with Missy. It was an unknown number.

"Hello," I answered in my perkiest voice. I didn't want to come off as angry or scornful. There was a silence for a moment. "Hello?"

"Hello, is this Paige?" a soft voice replied.

I sat back on my couch and propped my foot up. "Yes, this is."

"This is Taylor James. Missy just gave me your number."

I explained the entire situation to Taylor. She sat quietly while I told her all about my relationship with Kyra and why she was staying in my house, to begin with. I explained how I came home to find my house ruined and that I still had not heard from Kyra after bailing her out of jail and getting out of the hospital. She never interrupted, only let out a few *ohs* and *ahs* from time to time.

"Paige, I am so sorry about everything. I was unaware of the situation and had I known, I would never have been in your home. The only reason I came over was that Kyra called me hysterical, talking about she was thinking about harming herself. I've known her for a long time, and I know how she can get. But when I arrived, she just started trying to sleep with me and begging me to take her back. I told her that I was never coming back, and she got upset. She got so angry she started punching walls. When I tried to leave, she wouldn't let me, so I called the cops."

"Wow," I replied.

"Kyra has major issues. She is a fuckboy in a girl's body. I was tired of dealing with her and her drama. And finding out about Lisa was the final straw."

I thought about Lisa, the frumpy actual girlfriend. I wondered if she had also spent time in my house, or was Kyra staying away from her like her bail bondsman advised?

"Well, thank you for calling and being honest with me. It just feels weird being in my place knowing that I have no clue who all was here, who had access to my home."

"I understand. I won't let Kyra come to my house anymore. When we ended, she broke a very expensive vase that I loved. She's a mess, and I recommend you leave her with Lisa as they are equally fucked up."

"What do you mean?"

Taylor let out a little giggle. "Girl, Lisa puts up with all of Kyra's nonsense. They have physically fought in public so many times. When we found out about each other, she got mad at me, as if *I* knew anything about them. I think she's holding out hope that Kyra will become some major guitarist or something. Kyra will never be more than she is right now because she will always sabotage herself."

Taylor and I spoke about real estate for a little bit. I suddenly felt like a stranger in my own home. I didn't know if I wanted just to throw everything out or move. Taylor offered to assist if I decided to sell. I thanked her for taking the time to speak with me. We hung up, and I went back to snooping.

I found two other women having romantic and sexual conversations with Kyra. I couldn't help but feel slightly jealous. Kyra was saying such sweet things to them. Yet, I hadn't heard anything nearly as romantic from her in a long time. They were eating up her words the same way I had done several times. I wondered if Kyra used them the way that she had used me.

Self-pity set in. Why was *I* the one she chose to use? Why didn't *I* get the sweet, romantic words like the other women? Was I that gullible that I fell for everything, hook, line, and sinker? Then anger set in. I wanted revenge. I wanted Kyra to hurt the way she had hurt me. So I went back to the two women's DMs and began to type.

Hey, this is going to seem strange, but my name is Paige, and yes, I'm currently sending you a message from Kyra's Facebook. Why? Because the sloppy bitch left it open on my computer, in my house that she just recently destroyed. Not sure if you were one of the women Kyra entertained in my home, but I just thought you should know that *no*, I am *not* her straight friend. I was one of what seems to be multiple lovers. I trusted Kyra, and she used me and abused my home. I just thought you should all know that Kyra is full of shit. Don't let her stay with you, or your home will be demolished too.

I attached a few photos my aunt had taken of the mess in my home, copied the message, and sent it to both women. I didn't want to know their responses and didn't want to hear from them. I felt vindicated and was ready to move on. I thought about keeping Kyra's page open, but I knew it would only be a matter of time before she found out. So I logged out and closed the window. Behind the browser window was an open Microsoft Word document titled "Ramblings of a Muse."

Something told me not to read it, but I couldn't stop myself. I sat, mouth agape, as I read Kyra's writings.

Human behavior can be as complex as it is misleading. I don't know if I'll truly understand why God gave me this gift. I knew I should use my talents for good, but evil keeps calling me. At a young age, I learned that communication ruled the nation, and I was a gifted orator. The right words will charm a woman out of house and home just as I had done to Paige. I feel sorry for Paige. She wasn't the woman I wanted. But she isn't a bad person either. I was hurting a perfectly innocent and genuinely sweet human being. But she's also incredibly insecure and gullible, making it far too easy for me to use my gifts for evil. I knew from our first conversation she would be straight, bi, or whatever, but I could get her and get her to do anything I needed or wanted her to do. No, I wasn't attracted to her. Although she carries herself well, she's fat, insecure, and inexperienced. Sleeping with her makes me sick to my stomach. But she held me down, letting me get away with anything with little argument. Unlike Lisa, who I knew would never leave my side, I know Paige will come to her senses one day. But until that day comes, I will do whatever I want, damn the consequences. I know I'll have to answer for how I treat women one day. None of them deserved what I did. But they made it so damn easy, I couldn't help but do it.

Tears rolled down my face. I screamed as I slammed the computer closed and threw it across the room. It crashed into the wall. I didn't know if it was broken. I didn't care. I wanted something to feel as broken as I felt. As I sat there sobbing, I heard my phone chime a familiar sound. I looked at the phone to see a text message from Kyra.

I'm coming over in the morning to get my stuff.

Chapter 29

I sat in my chair, waiting for the doorknob to turn. Then someone knocked twice on the door. I yelled that it was open.

I had all night to stew in my feelings. I thought about telling my cousin. Word spread through my family about the state of my house. My cousin Latisha was the hood cousin and quickly called to tell me she would whoop Kyra's ass. All I had to do was say the word. I also thought about destroying all her little possessions. It wasn't like she had many of them and probably wouldn't miss them. But the Michelle Obama in me wouldn't let me stoop to the low places my mind was venturing to. I needed to handle this correctly.

Kyra walked in with some trash bags in her hand. Her head lowered with a sober expression covering her face. She didn't speak to me. She just began picking up her things from the couch. I watched as she stuffed all her belongings into the cheap plastic garbage bags, wondering if she would say anything. I noticed my headphones around her neck. My blood began to boil.

"So, are you really not going to say anything?"

"Ain't shit to say," she huffed.

"Are you fucking kidding me?" I wanted to jump up but knew it wasn't a good idea with my ankle.

Kyra paused. She turned to me. "What the fuck do you want me to say? That was some cold shit you did last night, Paige, and you know it."

I couldn't believe my ears.

"Are you *seriously* getting an attitude with me because I sent those messages? You ruined my fucking house! You *used* me!"

"Oh, Paige, I know you're a writer and all, but stop being so fucking dramatic." Kyra began stuffing her belongings into the bags again.

"I read your little journal entry. Glad to know how you *really* feel. I destroyed the computer, so, sorry. Guess you won't be able to get anything off it."

Kyra dropped a bag to the floor. She turned back toward me. We stared at each other as if we were about to duel. Then she shook her head.

"You would read a piece of fiction and take it as fact."

"You used my real name, Kyra. You literally can't be honest at all, can you?"

Kyra finished packing her things up and grabbed the three bags. "Yeah, I'm not doing this with you. Ain't no coming back from what you did yesterday. That was fucked-up. This is goodbye."

Kyra dropped my key on the table. I sat there frozen in disbelief as she walked out the door, slamming it in the process. And just like that, Kyra was out of my life. I had thought about how the conversation would go when I saw her a million times. But in none of those scenarios did I see her blaming *me* for everything.

I started to think about everything again. I wondered if the journal really was just her way of writing. Was it true, or just a work of fiction like she said? Had I jumped to conclusions based on the wrong thing?

"No!" I yelled as I furiously shook my head. I wasn't going to let her win this time. Regardless of the journal, I had seen the texts, and she had another woman in my house. Kyra had the opportunity to apologize but chose not to. She wouldn't take responsibility for anything she had done to me. But why should she? As she said, I was gullible and fell for all her bullshit. She used me, and I allowed her to.

An overwhelming sense of guilt and depression overcame me. I lay down on my couch and began to cry hysterically. I started to question everything about myself. All my terrible past relationships came back to my mind. I was like a big pot of honey attracting nothing but terrible bees trying to take advantage of whatever I offered. I wanted to be mad at Kyra, but I couldn't do anything but be mad at myself. I allowed all of this to happen.

For the next three days, I didn't leave my couch for anything besides going to the bathroom. I wasn't hungry. I smiled when my friends and family dropped off food or supplies, but the second they left, I went back into my shell of sorrow. I got to the point where I didn't want to pretend with my friends anymore. I didn't want to see anyone, but they were persistent.

Morgan and Tara sat on my love seat. They had arrived with three bottles of wine, determined to hang out. I continued lying on my couch, staring at the TV that was playing with the volume on mute.

"I mean, I just wanna fuck up the bitch." Tara broke the silence in the room.

"Fuck her. She doesn't deserve any more of your energy." Morgan stood up. She pulled some sage out of her purse. "I brought sage so we can banish her bad energy from your house. Hopefully, that will make you feel better."

"Fuck that. How about I just beat her ass? I think *that* will make you feel better." Tara crossed her arms. Her big boobs set up in her low-cut shirt. Tara's black braids had pops of bright colors of pink and purple throughout them. She was always ready to fight. This time, I really contemplated taking her up on the offer.

"I'm all right, you guys. I just feel really foolish." I sat up on my couch. "Like, why me? Why do these people always find me?"

Morgan and Tara didn't respond. Then finally, a tear fell from my eye. I quickly wiped it. I didn't want to cry anymore and especially not in front of my friends.

"Okay, so, truth moment." Tara shifted her body toward me. "You were a fool in love. It happens to everyone."

"Lord knows I've been a fool before," Morgan chimed in.

"Exactly. Remember how we felt when Morgan was dating Charla? Hell, let's not forget how I was over Galvin with his weak ass."

Morgan laughed. "Yes, I was dumb as fuck over Charla. And Galvin was the worst."

"Galvin was a fucking sociopath." Tara stood up. "That's it. Kyra is a fucking narcissistic sociopath."

I sat up. "What?"

Tara pulled out her phone. "Tell me, does this sound familiar?" She pulled up something on her phone. "A sociopathic narcissist will be cold and callous but will also be seeking the admiration of others (and will believe that they deserve it). As a result, they will have a disdain for people and think it's okay to exploit and dispose of others in what-ever way it helps them to get ahead."

My mouth dropped open. Morgan immediately agreed.

"That is Kyra to a tee. She didn't apologize. She's cocky, manipulative, selfish, condescending, and demanding. She had the nerve to come into my house after all she did and try to get an attitude with *me. That's* crazy."

"Yep, a sociopathic narcissist," Morgan replied.

"Aka, a fuck nigga, gender inclusive," Tara huffed and folded her arms.

We all laughed. I felt a tiny bit of happiness for the first time in a long time. Morgan walked over and sat next to me on the couch. She put her hand around me.

"Paige, don't feel bad. We have all been there. Just take it as a learning moment and move on from it. You will be bigger and better in no time, and Kyra will be miserable for the rest of her wretched life."

My friends kept me company for several hours. I was laughing and enjoying them to the point that I didn't want them to leave. I didn't want to go back to wallowing. I wanted my life back and felt a strong sense of determination to get it.

I wanted to move. I strapped on my boot and started to walk around my house with my walker. I didn't want the crutch anymore. Mario had already told me to start walking without the walker, promising me that I didn't need it. I pushed the walker out in front of me and started to attempt to walk on my own. The pain subsided as I moved around my house, staying close to the wall to ensure I was all right.

I finally decided to open the door to my bedroom. I turned on the light. It looked like my room, but something still felt off. Thoughts of Kyra and me having sex flooded my mind. I quickly tried to shake them off. I thought about the words in her journal. Sleeping with me made her sick. My stomach churned. Finally, I took a deep breath and closed the door. I never wanted to sleep in that bed again.

Chapter 30

I stood before a king-size, dark espresso panel bed with storage. It was the last of what seemed to be a million beds I had checked out. I needed a new bed but found something wrong with each one I saw.

"Okay, this is nice." Morgan bounced up and down on it. "Yeah, I like this one."

I winced. "I dunno. Maybe."

Morgan fell on her back and covered her face. "This is ridiculous. Just pick a damn bed already. I don't even know why you are buying a new bed, to begin with."

I didn't know what was causing my anguish. It had been a month since the incident, and I was finally starting to feel like myself again. I was still wearing my boot whenever I thought I would be on a big trip, but overall, I walked like an almost normal person again. A friend I knew was able to get me signed up with Obamacare, and they backdated my coverage to cover my entire hospital stay. So my eighty thousand debt went down to less

than five thousand. But I still couldn't sleep in my
bed. I couldn't get past the idea of women being in
my bed. I knew I couldn't sleep there, and I needed
to get a new one.

I hadn't heard from Kyra at all. I blocked her
on my social media and deleted her phone number. Even with Morgan's sage cleansing of the
house, the bedroom remained a sore spot for me.
If I couldn't find a new bed, my next option was to
move.

"Because, as of now, I know of multiple women
who have fucked in my bed. I have no interest in
sleeping in a bed or on a mattress soaked in random women's vaginal juices." I pushed down on
the mattress to check its firmness.

"Well, that was unnecessarily graphic." Morgan
frowned. "And still very unnecessary. Cleaning
the mattress and buying a new mattress cover and
sheets would still be way less than buying an entirely new bed set. Or just buy a new mattress. All
cheaper than a whole new bed set."

"You just don't get it."

"I get that you are going through something
and have reached the step in grieving when you
do stupid shit like spend thousands of dollars on
something you don't need." Morgan shrugged.

"Just answer, do you like the bed or not?"

"Yes, Paige, the bed is nice."

"Okay, fuck it. I'm getting this one." I motioned for the sales associate to come. She had been hovering over us the entire time. The older white lady perked up when I motioned for her. I could tell she was starting to think I wasn't a serious shopper.

"Hi, yes, so, what do you think?" Her high-pitched voice was annoying to me. I didn't know how she could sell to anyone.

"I'll take this one."

"Great. I'll start the order. You can meet me in the back." She swiftly walked away, probably hoping to get the sale before I changed my mind.

Morgan pulled herself off the bed, and we headed toward the back of the store. I walked, head lowered, checking out a few tables and other trinkets on our way to the back.

"I'm trying to be a supportive friend while you go through this emotional break. But can you tell me when you plan on seeking *real* help?"

"I don't think I've hit that rock bottom yet." I picked up the tag on a coffee table I liked.

"You've gone through a lot, and now you're buying a $4,000 bed. What next? A couch because if their pussy juices were on the bed, they might have had ass on the couch too?"

I froze. I had been sleeping on the couch and in my guest room and never thought that maybe Kyra had been fucking these women on my couch as well. Suddenly, my skin began to crawl. Morgan realized she fucked up telling me that.

"I'm sorry, girl. I was just—"

"Now I need a new fucking couch too. That's it. I can't be in my house right now. I'm moving out."

"So, let me take count. You're ready to replace damn near all your furniture and now possibly move out of your dream house, all over a bitch you were barely with, and yet, you don't think that maybe what you should do is just go talk to a therapist?" Morgan put her hand on my shoulder. "Paige, I love you, but please, don't buy any of this stuff. Talk to someone first. I know it can help."

I thought for a moment and knew Morgan was right. If there was ever a time to seek professional help, it was now. I didn't need new furniture, but I did need to escape for a while.

"Okay, let's get out of here before that saleslady realizes I'm not buying anything."

Suddenly, Morgan grabbed my arm and pulled me close.

"Bitch," she whispered, "that's Lisa."

I turned my head to see Kyra's main chick, Lisa, looking at a dining table set. I tensed up. I didn't want her to see me, but it was too late. We made eye contact. Her smile faded as she started walking toward us.

"Oh shit," I whispered under my breath.

"Just act natural. She might not know anything." Morgan held on to my arm. I figured that wasn't true from the look on Lisa's face.

"You're Paige, right?" Lisa approached us, gripping her purse for dear life.

"Yes. That's my name."

She held out her hand. "I'm Lisa. I figured we would run into each other at some point. Didn't expect it to be here." She looked at a couch near us. "I feel like we should have a little chat."

"Morgan, would you let the woman know I'm going to hold off for a while?"

"Um, yeah, sure." Morgan slowly walked away. I knew she was pissed she wasn't going to get to eavesdrop on the conversation. Lisa and I walked over to a couch and sat down. I was nervous. What did she know?

"So, I'm just gonna get right to the point." Lisa sucked her teeth. I hated that sound. "I know you and Kyra were more than what she claimed y'all to be. The girl couldn't tell the truth if her life depended on it."

"I'm sorry. I wasn't aware of you or the situation when Kyra and I started talking." I swallowed hard. I hadn't said her name in a while. So I started referring to her as "Voldemort" and "She-Who-Must-Not-Be-Named."

"Yeah, but you knew at some point. I mean, she left my house and came to your house. Very nice house, by the way. Yeah, I was in there a lot."

I didn't know if I wanted to laugh or punch her. It was apparent she was trying to assert some type

of dominance over me by throwing *that* dig my
way. But I remained calm. I still wasn't at 100 per-
cent, and the last thing I wanted was to have to
fight this girl in the store.

"Well, yeah, I figured you were in there . . .
amongst other women. Thus far, I only know
about three, well, four, now, including you."

I could tell my comment cut Lisa deeply, but
she tried not to show it. I didn't smile as much as I
wanted to. She tried to cut me, and I cut her right
back. I wasn't the one to play with, and she learned
quickly. She shifted her weight on the couch.

"There were others? I don't know how, considering I was always there," she shot back.

It was obvious I wasn't going to have a civil conversation with her like I did with the others. She
was angry, and rightfully so. I did know about her,
and I continued with Kyra anyway. I deserved the
anger she was throwing my way. But that didn't
change the fact that she also knew about me and
proceeded to mess with Kyra in *my* house. We
were both guilty and both stupid for allowing any
of it to happen. And I refused to let Kyra make me
even dumber by becoming a woman who argues
with other women over someone who played us
both. I wasn't going to let her have the upper hand,
but I would keep things civil. I needed to hold on
to my last piece of dignity.

I shrugged my shoulders. "Kyra found her ways. I talked to Taylor, but only DM'd the other two."

"Taylor . . ." Lisa froze. She swallowed. "*Taylor* was in your house?" My comment hit a nerve.

"Yeah, we talked for a while. Very nice. Actually, all of the women were very nice, considering the situation. But that's neither here nor there. So, again, I do apologize. But you don't have to worry about Kyra and me. I have no intentions of ever seeing her again."

I grabbed the couch arm so I could get up. Lisa put her hand on my leg.

"Thanks for the apology, but it's not needed. Plus, yeah, Kyra can kick rocks. I threw all her shit out. And she's begging me daily to come back, but I'm not thinking about her. But yeah, anyway, I told her never to call me again. But yet, she keeps blowing up my phone. She just won't let go. I'm sick of her shit. So you can have her. I don't want her."

"I think we both deserve better. But again, I hate that we need to have this conversation. And I do apologize for my part in hurting you in any way. I wish you the best."

Lisa didn't know how to respond. Behind her stern demeanor, I could see she was genuinely hurting. I had only dealt with Kyra for about a year. She had been dealing with Kyra and her foolishness for years. If it took me this long to get over

Kyra, I could only imagine what things would be like for her.

"Well, good luck on your recovery." Lisa slightly let her guard down.

"Have a good day."

I watched as Lisa walked out of the store. I knew she was upset. I figured she would get in the car and call Kyra immediately. Probably curse her out, fight her again, and possibly destroy some more items. But I also knew she was going right back to her. I felt sorry for her. I was her for a moment. I knew I never wanted to be her again.

Morgan joined me at the front door. I felt better than I had felt in a long time. Seeing Lisa and dealing with her attitude only further cemented that I never wanted to have anything to do with Kyra or anyone like Kyra again. I was in no rush to date again, but I knew that when I did, I would stop ignoring the red flags.

I was ready for more than a new bed. I wanted to start the next chapter in my life and leave the season of Kyra in my past.

Chapter 31

I stood with my cane in the middle of the large open space. I loved my house but knew I needed a change for a little while. The stained concrete floors looked freshly polished. A friend let me know her cousin was looking to sublet her loft for a few months while she would be teaching abroad. I jumped on the opportunity to see the fully finished place.

The loft was spacious but a definite change from owning my own home. I wasn't going to sell. I still loved my house, although it had been defiled. I wanted a change, and moving from my quiet neighborhood to the middle of downtown Memphis seemed like the perfect change I needed for a few months.

"So, what do you think?" Shelby walked back into the living room space. "I'm leaving everything but some of my clothes, so you will have most of the closet to yourself, and you don't need to bring any furniture. I do ask you to bring your own dishes, though. I love my dishes and would prefer they not be used." I could only consider her a hipster. She was taking a teaching contract assignment to teach for eight months in Tokyo. I was tempted to ask to join her.

"It's perfect. I'll take it."

I signed the paperwork and took possession of the keys. I was using the last of the new book advance to pay for it. Too bad I hadn't finished writing the book yet.

I got out of my Uber and headed back into my home. I was glad Morgan talked me out of the furniture. I did take her advice and had my mattress and couch steam cleaned. I bought a new mattress cover and threw out all my old sheets. Things were getting better, but I still couldn't shake the feeling of Kyra and her women in my home. The house was quiet. I tended to keep it that way. I spent most of my time getting lost in my thoughts. I took turns blaming Kyra and myself for my situation. I knew that she was the problem, but I also allowed her to do everything she did. I couldn't understand how I ever allowed myself to get into such a fucked-up situation.

I was doing better but not well enough. I found myself wondering about Kyra a lot. Did she miss me or even feel the slightest bit of remorse for how she treated me? I knew the answer, but I wanted to believe that maybe somewhere, she was thinking about me, even if it was just a little bit.

I spent even more time wondering how I allowed myself to get in such a shitty situation. I thought about my past relationships and how they weren't too much better. I asked myself why a lot. Why did I allow people to do these awful things to me? And what about me attracted people who didn't mean any good to me?

I knew moving was no different than running away, but I didn't feel comfortable in my house anymore. I thought about renting it on Air B&B, but the thought of more strangers in my space only made me even more uncomfortable.

I returned to my house to see my housekeeper packing my clothes. As much as I wanted to take things on my own, I didn't have the strength to do it. I had my good days and bad, but overall, the numbness just wouldn't go away.

Although things were better, I still couldn't completely shake this feeling of emptiness that filled me. I knew masking it with wine wasn't the answer. I needed to do something better. I took Morgan's advice and finally sought professional help. I sat across from Dr. Paula Dunnings, my new possible therapist. She was the third I had been to in less than a month. The first therapist was just too white and too hippy for me. The second, a man named Marshall, was nice, but I didn't want to deal with a man. A friend recommended Paula to me. She was a sister, natural and gorgeous. On her wall was a Basquiat print I had almost purchased for my home. She wasn't like the other therapists. She sat in a pair of jeans, some knee-high boots, and a T-shirt that said, *"Black Girl Magic."* Her natural hair was pulled back by a black and blue scarf. I liked her already.

"All right, Paige, so what brings you here today?"

The other two therapists had asked me the same question. I typically answered, "I need help getting over an ex." But today, I didn't want to say that.

"I need to figure out what is wrong with me that I keep attracting ain't-shit niggas and bitches into my life."

Paula smiled. "Well, that's straight to the point. I like it." She put down her iPad. "I'll need a little backstory. What makes you say that?"

I got comfortable on the couch and went in. I talked about my past, the women and men I had dated who had all done wrong to me. I went on and on about how everyone seemed to have negative intentions. Paula listened, taking in everything I was saying. I was rambling like word vomit flowed from my mouth. Finally, I made it to Kyra and my most recent situation. Paula never interrupted me. She let me get it all out. I didn't cry. I just explained the situation. I didn't know if I could cry anymore.

"All right," Paula responded when I finally said that was all. "So, yes, you have had quite a few traumatic experiences regarding dating. But I want to ask you a question, and I need you to take a moment and think about it before you respond."

"Okay."

"This is therapy for *you,* not for them. So focusing on what *they* did to you isn't going to help. My question is, why did you *allow* so much to go on? When the red flags appeared, why didn't you put an end to it before allowing them to do more?"

The question hit me like a freight train. I had asked myself the same question but never really answered it.

"Well, I try to give people a chance, but they always—"

"No." Paula stopped me. "That's about what *they* did. Again, why did *you* ignore the red flags?"

I was silent. I couldn't figure out how to answer without returning to what they did to me.

Paula continued. "Let's assess this last situation. Why did you accept her phone call again when she ghosted you the first time? Then when you went to her house, and she guilted you into sex on the floor, she told you then that you should leave. But you didn't. Why?"

I felt my body trembling. "Because . . ."

"Because what?" Paula leaned in. "Because *what,* Paige?"

"Because I didn't want to lose her." I didn't realize how loud I was. I felt tears starting to well in my eyes. "I wanted her so badly. I just wanted her. I didn't want to lose her."

"But do you realize you were afraid to lose someone that never had been yours, to begin with?" Paula's calm tone read me like a book. She handed me a box of Kleenex.

"I thought she would be mine."

"You wanted her to, but she showed you almost from day one that she wasn't what you needed or wanted. In fact, most of the people you mentioned showed you the same thing. But you ignored it. Why? *That* is what I want us to explore. You can't sit and focus on what they did because people only do what you allow them to do. That might sound harsh, but I believe in shooting straight from the hip. So for our time here, we will work on *you* and figure out *your* need to be stronger in these situations."

"You think I have low self-esteem, don't you?" I muttered.

"I think you have some deeply rooted insecurities that appear when you meet these individuals. You have this 'lone wolf' persona that you live by, but when someone comes into your life, you fight for dear life to keep them, even when you know you don't need them. You cling on to the small bits of good they show and ignore the tons of bad. So, first, you need to be okay with being honest with yourself. You don't want to be a lone wolf. You want to be loved. Which is a perfectly normal way to feel."

"Well, shit, Dr. Paula, you really didn't need to read me like that." I crossed my arms.

"That's my job. My job is to help you uncover your truths and help you do the work to fix anything that needs fixing. Paige, it's okay to realize that not everyone deserves a chance. Not everyone is worthy of being in your space. When you let negative forces into your world, they chip away pieces of you. I want us to work on fixing those pieces and making you whole so that these situations don't keep repeating themselves."

I sat back on the couch and wiped the tears from my eyes. I knew she was right, but I didn't want to accept it completely. There had to be something more than it just being what I allow.

"But you didn't answer my question. Why do you think these people seem to gravitate to me? Am I putting off desperate energy or something? Is it that they see this fat girl and immediately think that I'm easy prey?"

Paula sat back in her chair with her lips pressed firmly together. She stared at me with the same calm expression on her face. Then she crossed her legs.

"Paige, you are doing it again. You're focusing on the people and not on you."

"But could you just answer my question?"

"I'll answer the question for you, but answer something for me first."

I folded my arms and rolled my eyes. I was already thinking of finding another therapist once I left.

"Tell me, Paige, how many books have you published?"

"I have six books published," I said with attitude. I wanted her to know how annoyed I was.

Then she shook her head. "No, that can't be right."

"Why do you say that?"

"Because fat people are lazy slobs who don't do anything besides eat. No way you wrote six books."

"*Excuse* me?" I felt my blood boiling before it hit me. I knew what she was doing, and by the smile on her face, Paula knew it too.

"So to answer your question, yes, some people will see your size and think you have low self-esteem, easy to get over on, and so desperate to be loved that you will accept anything. But just like you prove that all fat people are not lazy, you must prove that you are not any of those other things as well. And from what you have told me, you haven't quite figured that out yet."

She was right, even if I didn't want to admit it.

Chapter 32

I sat in the office with Paula. It was my seventh session, and I was becoming more and more comfortable with her each time. I looked forward to seeing how her hair would change and what type of cool dope saying would be on her shirt with each visit. This time, she opted for two cornrows braided to the back and a shirt that read, "*Normalize Therapy.*"

"I just don't think that there is anything wrong with holding people accountable for their actions," I said, leaning back on the chaise lounge in her office. It had become my new favorite place to sit since it allowed me to kick up my feet.

"You're right. You are able to hold people accountable, but only in your life." Paula stood up and walked over to her small fridge. She pulled out two mini-bottles of water and headed back toward us. "But the problem with accountability, especially in your case, is the follow through." She handed me a bottle before sitting down.

"I guess." I took a sip.

"You can ask anything you want of a person. They also have the choice to do what you ask of them. They can also chose not to. The question is, what is your response going to be when they don't give you what you are asking for?"

I sat for a moment and pondered what she said. I thought about Kyra and other relationships of my past. So many times I begged and pleaded with people to give me basic common respect, and yet, they never did. But I knew I never really held them accountable for those actions. I just bitched a little and got over it, allowing them to continue the things that I didn't like. I was a pushover, and I hated myself for it.

"Uh-oh, where did you go just then?" Paula asked, picking up on the quick change in my demeanor.

"I'm just realizing that you're right. *I* am the problem."

"Now, don't put words in my mouth. It's not about one person or the other being the problem. It's about not focusing on the other person and just focusing on yourself. We can't change other people. We can only change ourselves and how we react to them."

There was another silence between us. I had been doing so well not thinking about Kyra. Life was finally feeling normal again. I was loving downtown living. I spent many nights hanging out at local spots right in my neighborhood. I didn't need my cane anymore, although I still kept it in my car just in case I felt I might need it. I was actually enjoying time with my friends instead of merely tolerating them just to appease their need to check on me. I was writing again and not hating everything that I came up with. And in one session, I was back with Kyra on my mind.

"Kyra."

"Ah, you haven't said that name in a few sessions." Paula sat back and crossed her legs. "What do you think triggered her in your mind?"

"I think it's just everything we've been working on has been great, but I can't get past one thing. The why. It's like unfinished business. Like I need closure."

"Well, if you need closure, go get it." Paula sat up straight in her chair. "You know her number and where to find her. Go out and get it."

"You can't be serious."

"Hey, if that's what you truly think you need, go do it. But my question is, what are you going to do if she doesn't give you the answers that you want? The last time you saw her, she threw everything on you. She didn't take responsibility for anything. So, if you go and ask for this closure, and she doesn't give it to you, how are you going to go on from there?"

I made it home with my session still on my mind. I turned my Bluetooth speaker on and went straight to the "Moving On" playlist I made on

Spotify. Jasmine Sullivan's "Forever Don't Last" filled my loft. It was not the song I needed to hear in that moment. I sat on the couch absorbing the lyrics as Jasmine belted them out. Forever didn't last long, but in my case, forever never even started.

I pondered what Paula said to me. She was right. I could walk out of the house now and go to one of three spots and easily find Kyra. I could walk up to her and demand she explain everything to me. I could go on her social media, which I had finally deleted, and easily find out exactly where she would be. I could cause a scene, tell the entire world how she fucked me over. But all I wanted to know was why. Why she chose me? Why she entered my life and took advantage of me for no apparent reason. Why, if she respected me as an author of books that she claimed she loved, would she betray me and disrespect me and my home? I didn't want to cause a scene.

I thought about the things I read on my computer that she wrote. I really had all the answers right there on my computer. But I still didn't understand why. What about me made her decide I was the easy mark? She had plenty of fans, plenty of women who wanted just a few moments of her time. Women who she could easily have one-night stands with and go on her way. But she chose me. She made the conscious decision to fuck up the ability to have a friendship with me only to treat me like trash, and for that, I just couldn't wrap my head around it. I thought about that first conversation on New Year's Eve. We could have been great friends; we could have hung out without any romantic involvement at all. At least then, we would be in each other's lives. But instead, she ruined everything. And I would never know why . . . Or would I?

I picked up my phone, scrolled to her name and pressed the message icon. I stared at the screen, seeing our last text encounters. I scrolled all the way back to the first time she ever texted me, back when I thought she was the one. I shook my head, I wasn't going to allow myself to do that. There would be no reminiscing about when things were good. Because the truth was, they never were. And I wanted to know why. I knew I needed to follow my therapist's advice. What would I do if she didn't respond or give me the answers that I so desperately needed. I knew there was only one way to find out. I typed four words.

We need to talk.

Chapter 33

A week had passed with no response from Kyra. I knew it was a long shot, but I decided to take it anyway. I sent the text and waited for a reply. I stared at the screen, hoping to at least see the three dots letting me know she was typing, but there was nothing. She never opened my message. I decided to call it a night. I would take the week to work on moving on without the closure I wanted. It was the best thing to do.

I picked up my MacBook and opened a blank document. A rush of energy came over me. I started typing. Our entire fucked-up affair flooded back like a movie playing in my mind. I started writing it all down. New Year's Eve, her birthday, our sexual experiences, my birthday. Everything was coming back in vivid details, and I wrote it all. Two days passed, and all I did was eat, sleep, and write. Chapter after chapter, I relived the entire relationship. I held nothing back. I cried, laughed, and cringed at just how stupid I really allowed myself to be for Kyra. By the end of four days, I had finished the entire first draft of the book.

As I pressed The End, it felt as if a giant weight had lifted off me. I took a deep breath and exhaled all of the bullshit of Kyra. It felt good. I had never been so honest in any of my work. I knew I had to change names, and this was completely different from any of the books I had written in the past. This wasn't a love story. It was a real story.

I was headed back to work in three weeks and decided to throw myself into my writing before I had to work again. Things were flowing better than I could have even imagined. By the end of the time, I had edited my new novel and turned it in to my publisher.

It was my final weekend before going back to work. My publisher requested a zoom meeting with me. I was nervous, as he never asked for a zoom meeting before. It had been a week since I turned in the novel. I didn't think a zoom could mean anything but bad news. My mind went to the worst place. Were they going to drop me because they hated the book that much? It was drastically different from what I had written in the past. Would they refuse to publish it?

At the designated time, Mark's face appeared on my computer screen. I scanned the background of his video. I always wondered what his house looked like. The room was a dark blue. He sat in front of a shelf with all types of awards sitting on it. I was impressed.

"Paige, I don't want to keep you long, but I just needed to give you a call. Read your book." I couldn't read the expression on his face. I had no idea how this was going to go.

"Wow, that was fast." I tried to make light of the situation, but I was a ball of nerves.

"Yeah, well, I was surprised when I got it. Didn't expect anything so soon, especially since you had all that stuff going on with the hospital. How are you, by the way? Did you get the flowers we sent you?"

"Yes, they were lovely. Thank you." I tried not to sound anxious.

"Well, let me stop rambling. Paige, so, this book . . . I personally believe it is the best thing you have ever written."

My mouth dropped open. "Wait, what? Are you serious?" I covered my mouth.

"I don't know where this came from, but you pulled it from somewhere different, and it worked. It worked so much that I am fast tracking this book and putting a full promotion behind it. I'm talking tours, interviews. I see *New York Times* in your near future."

"I really don't know what to say," I said as I put my hands on my head. I felt like I was dreaming.

"Just get ready. You did a fantastic job, Paige. I have another meeting, but I will be in touch again next week. Congratulations again."

We disconnected the zoom. I sat staring at the computer. I couldn't believe it. A burst of giddiness filled my body. I jumped up and screamed, "Yes!" throwing my fist in the air.

I headed straight to the liquor store to buy myself an expensive bottle of champagne. Then I stopped by my favorite bakery and bought a mini-cake for myself. I ordered my favorite pizza and decided to have a private celebratory party for me. I thought about calling my friends to share the good news but decided I wanted relish in the moment by myself for a little while. Not only was it shaping up to be a major accomplishment for me, but with the book, I was closing a chapter in my life, and closing the door on Kyra with it.

I pulled into my gated parking spot and grabbed my treats. I was going to enjoy my favorite things. A few minutes later, the delivery guy arrived with my New York Style Cheese Pizza from my favorite pizza spot. I admired the spread I had sitting on the coffee table. It was all unhealthy, and I didn't care. I was going to watch cheesy romantic comedy and chill, one of my favorite pastimes, and just be happy.

Suddenly, my phone rang. The vibration caused my cake box to tumble to the ground. I let out a scream as the box fell over on its top. I groaned, knowing my cake was ruined. I let out a sigh before shrugging my shoulders. Oh well, it would be eaten regardless.

I put the pizza down on the counter and picked up my phone to see who the missed call was from. I figured it was one of my friends. They always called at the worst moments at times. When I looked at the screen, I froze, I had deleted her name, but her number was etched in my brain. It was Kyra.

I contemplated if I should call her back. Suddenly, I got angry. Here I was about to celebrate the closing of that chapter in my life, and she finally wants to pop her head back in. I was over it and decided not to call her back. Just then, my phone rang once more. It was her again. I let out a long sigh and answered.

"Hey." Her raspy voice echoed through my speaker. Wherever she was, a lot was going on in the background. I wondered if she had me on speakerphone too. Was this another way to humiliate me, call me to see if I'm going to say something to make her look good? I wasn't going to give her the satisfaction.

"Hi," I said in a dry tone.

"I'm sorry. I've been stupid busy and not really checking my texts. I saw where you texted me earlier this week and decided it probably would be easier just to call. Is everything all right?"

I froze. She sounded concerned and almost sincere, as if nothing had transpired between us. Was she *that* conceited to think that she could just call me as if nothing had ever happened? I honestly knew she was.

"It's nothing. Don't worry about it." I sat down on my couch. I knew I had two choices. I could tell her that yes, I wanted to talk to her, or I could continue with closing that chapter and just let it go.

"You sure?" Kyra asked. "Your message said we needed to talk. And honestly, I agree."

I was dumbfounded. What could she possibly have to say to me? Was she going to apologize like she should have done back then, or was this some type of ploy to see if she still could get me if she wanted me?

"Yeah, well, I don't think it's that important anymore. It's all good." I instantly regretted my choice of words. It wasn't all good at all.

Only the sound of her loud background blared through the phone for a moment. I wondered what she would say next.

"Paige, I would love the opportunity to talk to you. Listen, I'm downtown at The Blue Monkey right now. But I could be in Midtown in an hour."

I wanted to scream. She was literally around the corner from my new place, and she didn't even know it. I had the opportunity to get her face-to-face and ask her the questions I had been wondering about since we ended. I could hear Paula's voice in my head. What if she didn't give me the answers I was hoping for? Suddenly, I got a strange feeling in the pit of my stomach. What if she *did* give me the answers I wanted? What would I do then?

I sighed. "Actually, I have a place downtown now. I'm on Mulberry, right across from the National Civil Rights Museum." I instantly regretted saying that.

"Oh shit, that's right around the corner. Do you mind if I come by?"

I didn't respond. I had to think, and I had to think fast. I knew all my friends would tell me hell no, do not let that energy that I worked so hard to get rid of invade my new place.

"Actually, I can just come to the Blue Monkey," I replied.

Kyra paused for a moment. "Paige, it's really loud here, and I think we need something a little less crowded. I promise I won't be long. Will you allow me to come over? Please?"

I don't think I had ever heard her say please before.

"I'll text you the address."

Chapter 34

I sat on my couch waiting on Kyra to call me so I could open the gate. There was no getting ready for her this time. I didn't care to put on any of my body splash or scented lotions. I wasn't going to obsess over the right outfit. She was going to get me in my distressed jeans and Sailor Moon T-shirt I had been rocking all day. The days of me preparing for her were long gone. Then my phone rang.

"Hey, so, I think I'm here," Kyra said, almost sounding like she was whispering in the phone.

I stood up and walked over to my door. I could see her standing outside the gate. I wondered if she walked over here or if she was in some other unsuspecting female's car.

"I'll open the gate."

I pressed my gate remote and opened the front door. Kyra walked in. I don't know why I expected her to look different, but she still looked the same. But my rose-colored glasses were gone. I could see her for what she really was. Her jeans had rips in them and looked like they hadn't been washed in months. Her shirt was way too big and had a hole in the bottom that wasn't there for fashion purposes. Her hair, pulled in her man bun, was sloppy and needed to be brushed. But even with all the flaws, she still looked good.

I didn't move, I wasn't going to give her a warm welcome hug. She admired the area as she made it to my door.

"This is nice, Paige. When did you move here?"

"Not too long ago," I replied as she approached the door.

"Oh, you selling your crib?"

"Naw, I just, needed a change for a little while."

We were standing face-to-face. Kyra looked me in my eyes. I immediately looked away and walked into the house. She followed, closing the door behind her.

"Well, this is dope; a fantastic location. But I wouldn't expect you not to be in something nice."

"You can have a seat," I said moving right past her compliment.

She sat on the couch, and I sat in my oversized chair. Netflix's screensaver scrolled on my television, showing different shows and movies on the app. Kyra pointed to the screen.

"Have you watched that movie yet? It was pretty good."

"Kyra, why?" I blurted out, ignoring her attempt at casual talk. I didn't need to talk about movies with her. I wanted my answers, and I wanted her gone. "I just-I really just would like to know why you did me the way you did."

Kyra dropped her head. "Just getting right into it I see. Okay, I know I deserve that." She pressed her palms against each other. "Yeah, so, I really don't know how to explain that."

"Well, try." I sat still, lips pressed tightly together.

Kyra sighed. She put her hands on each side of her head. She looked like she was in anguish as she looked over at me.

"Paige, I know you aren't going to believe me, but the last thing I ever planned to do was hurt you. I really respect you as a woman, artist, and friend. I just . . ." Kyra stood up. "It's like I was a tornado of fucked-up-ness, and you got caught in the path of it. And I am really sorry about that."

I shook my head. I heard what she was saying, but it wasn't adding up.

"No offense, but you're right. That sounds like bullshit. If you knew you were in this bad space, why hit me up in the first place? Why jeopardize the friendship we could have had to treat me like shit?"

"Because I was fucked up. I wasn't shit. I can admit to that."

"Now," I folded my hands, "you can admit to that now. Because last time you saw me, after you destroyed my house, all you could do was point your finger at me as if *I* were the problem."

Kyra shook her head and let out a laugh. "Ah, yeah. That. I mean, you really did me in, girl. I know not to cross you again."

My blood began to boil. "I did *you* in? No, Kyra, I didn't do anything besides try to find out who was in my house. I could have done so much worse. And I thought about it too. I thought about it a lot. But for some reason, I decided to take the high road."

"That's because you, Paige, are genuinely a good person. I cannot say the same for myself." Kyra's voice lowered as she sat back on the couch. "I am fucked-up, Paige. I am working to fix that, but it is what it is. I'm fucked-up. But I am sorry. I truly apologize for way I treated you."

Silence filled the room. I could see the pain in her eyes, and my anger subsided. Suddenly, all the questions I had faded. I didn't need to ask anything else. Paula was right. There was nothing she could say that would make me happy. She was sitting on my couch, almost in tears, telling me that she was sorry, and it still wasn't good enough for me. I realized I didn't need her apology after all.

"Kyra, you are a talented human, but yeah, you are also deeply fucked-up. You hurt me in a way I never expected. I literally moved out of my house. I couldn't be there because of what you did. But you are right. Only a deeply damaged person would do something so fucked up to a person who truly cared about them. And you didn't do it just to me. You did it to others too. I hope you are getting the help that you need."

"Paige, I will never be able to take back the things I did. But I just want you to know that I do hate that we ended the way we did. I know I don't deserve it, but I hope that we will be able to at least be friends at some point. We could be great friends, don't you think? I could really use a good friend."

I thought about her words. I thought about all the good times we had just hanging out, watching movies, and talking. Could we have that again, or did too much happen that we would never be able to get past? I wanted to hate her. I spent so much time trying to hate her, but I couldn't. Even in that moment, I couldn't stay mad. I felt sorry for her.

"Maybe. One day."

Silence filled the room again. Kyra looked up at the TV.

"Sooo, did you watch that new Netflix show?" A small grin appeared on her face, her deep right dimple inset.

I couldn't help but to smile. "Of course I did."

Kyra and I shared pizza and watched a Netflix movie together. She told me about upcoming gigs and the opportunity she got to play for a celebrity's birthday party.

"So, have you gotten any writing done?" she asked as she stuffed a piece of pizza in her mouth.

"Actually, yes. And I got some really fantastic news about it today." I took a sip of water. I decided liquor was a bad idea with Kyra around, and for the first time, she didn't ask for any.

Kyra's eyes widened. "Word? Are you going to tell me what it's about?"

I hesitated. I didn't expect to ever see Kyra again, so I never thought I would have to tell her about the book. I knew I could just hide it, let her find out the subject matter when the world found out. But the petty part of me wanted to know her feelings.

"You might not like the subject."

Kyra sat back on the couch. "Oh shit, it's about me?"

"It's really about me. But it is loosely based off our situation," I lied. It was almost a complete play-by-play of our relationship. "But don't worry. Names were changed to protect the guilty." I smiled.

Kyra shrugged her shoulders. "You know what, if my fucked-up-ness leads to a bestseller for you, then I'm cool with it. At least something good should come from the mess I created."

"Ah, something we can both agree on."

We both laughed.

I walked Kyra to the door. We stood in the doorway for a moment, neither knowing what we should do next.

"Well, thank you, Paige, for inviting me over. I really appreciate you taking the time to at least hear me out."

"No problem."

"Can I?" Kyra spread her arms. I thought about it for a moment. Watching a movie on two separate pieces of furniture was one thing, but embracing in any way . . . I wasn't sure about that. "Come on; please, don't leave me hanging."

I walked closer, and Kyra wrapped her arms around me. The familiarity of her was gone. The hug lingered. She held on tight. I wrapped my arms around her, hugging her back, causing her to hold me even tighter.

"You are a phenomenal woman, Paige Writes. I'll hit you later."

I watched as she walked out of my gate. I closed the gate behind her, knowing that would be the last time my gate ever opened for her. I walked back into my house, grabbed my bottle of champagne chilling in my freezer, and popped the cork. I took a drink directly from the bottle. This was something to truly celebrate. I was officially over Kyra.

Chapter 35

"So, how do you feel?"

I sat on Paula's chaise. She was stirring a cup of tea with a small spoon. Her shirt of the day said, *"Unapologetically Dope"* with her hair down in a curly 'fro.

I smiled. "Honestly, I feel good. I know you didn't want me to reach out, but something told me I needed to. And I'm happy with the outcome."

"So, you feel you got the closure you were looking for?"

I shook my head. "No, I realized with her sitting there that I didn't need closure from her at all. It was weird, but having her there showed me that I was good after all. I was holding on to something I didn't need at all."

"Interesting." Paula nodded her head. "So, where do you go from here? Because the thing we know you struggle with is . . ."

"I know. Not making people do things and allowing them to stay in my life. I don't think that is happening here. When she left, I honestly didn't think I ever needed to see her again. But I'll be okay if we end up in the same room one day, which we probably will."

Paula put down her cup. "Listen, I love what you are saying. But only time will tell with the follow-through. I don't know her, but it sounds like Kyra has some deeply rooted issues she needs to deal with. She might be making some strides in correcting her behavior or still be full of shit. Only time will tell. That's not my concern. My concern is that you keep your eyes open to red flags and do not repeat past mistakes. That you remember that you set what you will and won't allow in your life, and you don't make concessions to that."

"You're absolutely right. I promise I won't." I smiled.

"Well, like I said," Paula picked up her cup again, "only time will tell."

I left Paula's office feeling oddly liberated. I felt fantastic about all the progress I had made. I realized I didn't feel like my old self. Instead, I felt like a new me—a better me.

I decided to treat myself to some new clothes. I thought about buying some sexy new number but realized that wasn't me. So instead, I headed to Torrid and bought myself an Avengers shirt and a Harry Potter one. Finally, I was done with people trying to turn me into what they felt I needed to be. I liked my jeans and T-shirts, and I wasn't going to let anyone else shame me from wearing them.

I made it home and decided I would start a new Anime series on Crunchyroll. I decided I needed one more week before starting work, but that was ending. I was sent notes from my editor, which I was able to work on during the week. I took meetings with a few publicists and picked the one I liked the most. Things were coming together. I was headed back to work on Monday, leaving the weekend to enjoy myself before returning to work. I was going to spend it doing exactly what I wanted . . . watching Anime and playing video games.

By Saturday night, I was deep into my nerd fest. I could hear the sounds of downtown from my window. It was a typical night in downtown Memphis. A party of bikers was blaring its music, undoubtedly filled with drunken women, as it passed my street. The roaring of motorcycles annoyed me, making it hard to hear my game. I took a break from *Demon Slayer* and decided to play some video games. I was deep into my *Grand Theft Auto*. I turned the sound up, hoping to drown out some outside sounds. I suddenly missed my old home and almost packed my game and headed back to it. But I knew things would calm down soon.

I took a break from my game to grab some water when my phone rang. It was after midnight, and I knew none of my friends would call me this late, thinking I was probably already in bed. I walked over and grabbed my phone. Kyra's face appeared.

I had added her back to my contacts and instantly regretted it. I decided to ignore the call and sat back down to get back to my game. But my phone started ringing again. I ignored it, only for it to begin ringing one more time. I finally answered it.

"Yes, Kyra."

"I'm sorry, is this Paige?" a woman replied.

"Um, yes. Who is this?" My heart dropped. I braced myself, knowing this must be one of Kyra's women calling to find out who I was or to see if we were involved.

"I'm sorry to bother you. My name is Susan. I'm friends with Kyra," the woman replied. She sounded very British and very white.

I picked up my controller. "Um, okay. How can I help you?"

"Again, I'm so sorry to bother you. I'm with Kyra, and we are outside of your house. She's a bit sloshed and told me to bring her here."

"Excuse me?" I stood up and rushed to my door. I looked out to see a car parked in front of my gate. "Why did she tell you to do that?"

"Well, my boyfriend and I were only in town for a few hours. We have to return our rental and catch our flight. She got a bit too drunk, and when I asked her where to take her, she said here."

"Paige! Paige Writes. Lemme in!" Kyra's voice echoed through the phone.

"I'm sorry, but I don't have time to take her anywhere else, or we're going to miss our flight. Would you mind terribly just letting her in? At least she could call an Uber or something."

I wanted to scream. This is why I should never have let her come over in the first place. After one good conversation, she's trying to use my house as her crash pad.

"Um, I don't know."

"Paige," Kyra's voice slurred. "Please, let me in. Please, babe."

"Please, Paige, I know I don't know you, but I don't want to leave her on the street," Susan begged. I pushed the button and watched the gate open. "Thank you so much. You are wonderful."

I watched as Kyra stumbled up the parking lot to my door. The cute little white woman waved at me as she got in the passenger seat. They didn't wait on Kyra to get in the house before driving off. So I was stuck with her.

"Paige. Thank you, Paige." Kyra slurred. I had never seen her this drunk before.

"Kyra, sit down. I'm going to make you some coffee. Give me your phone, so I can call you an Uber."

Kyra plopped down on my couch. She flipped off her shoes and lay down. "I can't call Uber right now. Just let me have a moment to rest. I know you don't want me here. You don't want me anymore."

I ignored her as I walked into the kitchen, where I pulled out a Keurig pod and fixed her a cup of coffee.

"You don't love me anymore, Paige. I fucked up. I fucked up, baby." Kyra's voice trembled as she slurred her words. I threw a creamer in the coffee and brought it over to her.

"Drink this." I tried to block out what she was saying. I didn't want to hear that stuff. I looked down to see Kyra's eyes closed. "Kyra."

"Just-just let me rest my eyes for a moment. Please."

I rolled my eyes as I grabbed a throw off my chair. I covered her with it. Then I grabbed the trash can from my bathroom and set it by the couch. The last thing I wanted to do was end up cleaning her vomit. I realized my nerdy night was officially over. I turned my game off and turned off the lights in the loft. Finally, I crawled into bed. It was past my bedtime anyway.

Deep in my sleep, I felt something touch my shoulder. I woke up to see a shadowy figure standing inches away from me.

"Kyra." I went to sit up, but she put her finger on my lips. She didn't speak. Then she leaned in and pressed her lips against mine.

Chapter 36

I knew I didn't need to do it, but I couldn't help it. Kyra pulled the covers off my bed. Then she pulled my leg toward her, making her way onto my bed. I knew I needed to stop her, but something wouldn't let me.

She grabbed the back of my head, pulling me into her. My mouth fell open as I allowed her to kiss me again. Her tongue danced against mine. I could taste the coffee. This wasn't a drunken moment. She was very alert and aware of what she was doing.

There were no words. There in the darkness, Kyra pulled my shirt over my head. I didn't have on any underwear, giving her easy access to me. Why didn't I wear more clothes to bed? Did I subconsciously prepare for this just in case it happened? My vagina began to throb as her index finger pressed against my clit.

"Damn, you're so wet." Kyra's low gasp caught me off guard as she rubbed circles around my clit. Then her two middle fingers entered me. She traced the curves in my hip with her fingertips as our lips met again for another fiercely passionate kiss. I arched my back as she worked her dark magic on me. She was very familiar with my body and hadn't forgotten a single inch of me.

Kyra's lips made their way down my neck, arriving at my left breast. She pressed her lips around my hard nipple and nibbled on it gently. I pushed my pussy up, pushing her fingers deeper inside. Her teeth grazed my swollen areola as her tongue swirled around it. I didn't realize how much I needed it, even if it was from her. I wanted more. I deserved more.

I raised my hand, placing it on Kyra's bun. Then I grabbed the bun with my hand and pushed her head down. Kyra followed my lead, the tip of her tongue licking my inner thigh. Next, she kissed my southern lips before her tongue parted them. Kyra's lips wrapped around my clit. She pressed down, sending a jolt of energy through my entire body. Her tongue stroked my clit as her fingers committed the most pleasurable assault inside my pussy. She pulled her fingers out, licking my essence off her two middle fingers. Immediately afterward, she grunted as her mouth dug deeper into me.

I arched my ass as Kyra's tongue entered inside me. Whimpers of euphoria escaped my mouth as Kyra's tongue fucked me into a frenzy. My body was reaching its peak as she devoured me. Her hands gripped both my ass cheeks, pulling them up, making sure she got as deep as she could. I slowly pushed my pussy against her mouth, causing the intensity to skyrocket. My body began to tremble. I thrust my ass up as Kyra's lips pressed firmly against my clit. My trembling legs wrapped around her face. She didn't miss a beat. Kyra sucked and licked, devouring me until the fire reached its peak, causing my body to jerk. Caught in the rapture, I erupted with Kyra enjoying every drop. Finally, I couldn't take anymore. My legs went limp, and my body betrayed me, giving it up so freely to her. But I couldn't be mad. It was what my body craved, and it got what it wanted.

"Damn, girl." Kyra fell beside me. She kissed my back as she pulled me into her. Her arms wrapped around me, our bodies pressed tightly against each other. Finally, we fell asleep.

Chapter 37

I woke up with Kyra's arms still wrapped around me. Slowly, I pulled my body away, getting out of bed as quietly as possible. She was knocked out and didn't feel me move at all. I walked to my bathroom and looked in the mirror. I knew last night should never have happened, but I couldn't help but enjoy it.

I took a shower and wrapped my towel around my body. Then I grabbed my robe and slipped my slightly damp body inside it. I didn't want to think about what had happened. It was a moment of weakness that led to a night of pleasure. Was that so wrong?

I knew it was, but I didn't care at that moment. I covered my body in pear body butter before putting on my underwear and bra. Finally, I grabbed a pair of leggings and a T-shirt and got dressed. As I pulled up my leggings, I heard the rustling of my sheets.

"Hey, you." Kyra's morning voice greeted me as she rubbed her eyes.

"Morning."

"A good morning it is. Thank you for letting me crash last night. I really appreciate it."

I nodded my head as I pulled my T-shirt over my head.

I made coffee and cooked a few pieces of turkey bacon while Kyra showered. She came out wearing the same clothes she had on the night before. Then she sat at the kitchen table and pulled out her phone.

"I ordered a Lyft. It's about to pull up. That smells good," she said, not looking up from her phone.

"Here." I handed her a tumbler of coffee and two pieces of bacon wrapped in a paper towel.

Kyra took a sip of coffee and bit a piece of bacon. Then she let out a moan. "Man, this is hitting the spot right now. Thank you, Paige."

We walked to the door. Kyra pulled me close and wrapped her arms around me. I embraced her. "Be safe out there," I whispered in her ear.

"Always," Kyra replied. She pressed her lips against my forehead. "Thank you again for last night."

I looked at the woman I thought would be my forever as she walked down to the gate. I had been a fool for her for so long. And in one night, I allowed her back in, something I said over and over that I would *never* do again.

Kyra opened the door to the Lyft. She paused, turning her head back to me. "Call you later?"

I looked at her, her messy hair pulled back into a low ponytail. I stood in my doorway, knowing I needed to tell her never to contact me again. She stood there like a giant red flag, the red flag I ignored so many times, and that had almost ruined me. I knew I needed to tell her never to contact me again. I needed to close my door, go back to my house, delete her number, and block her again on my social media. I did not need to let her back into my world. I stood there looking at her as she awaited my reply.

"Yeah, call me later."

The End

Notes